SUMMER
OF THE
WOODS

By Steven K. Smith

MyBoys3 Press

For more information, contact us at:

MyBoys3 Press, P.O. Box 2555, Midlothian, VA 23113

www.myboys3.com

Library of Congress Control Number: 2013910120

Third Printing

ISBN: 978-0-9893414-1-7

To Matthew, Josh and Aaron,
for all our adventures yet to come –
in and out of the woods

CONTENTS

SUMMER
OF THE
WOODS

ONE
THE WOODS

In the long hot summers of central Virginia, the trees danced at night. Inside the old white house with the black shutters, two boys watched the towering silhouettes rock in the breeze outside their bedroom window through the moonlight. The brothers shared a room and talked back and forth to each other in their beds, trying to keep themselves from falling asleep like all boys do. When they grew tired of talking and laughing, they lay still and listened to the wind moving through the high trees all around their house, moaning like an old train slowly chugging through the darkness.

It was the second week of June and the school year was over early since only a few snow days had been used over the winter months. A seemingly endless summer vacation lay ahead of them. The air was getting hot and the days were long, stretching far into the evening. Derek and Sam had just moved with their parents from up north to Virginia the week before. They'd said goodbye to their friends and their school and followed the moving truck on the long drive down the interstate highway.

One of the things that had excited them most about moving into their new home, despite having to leave all they knew behind, was the deep woods that lay past their backyard. So as their parents unpacked the house, the boys began to venture outdoors.

At first, the dark woods were a little scary for Sam, who was eight, and Derek, who was ten. But as the boys cautiously began to explore this new uncharted world, their young minds started to dream about the adventures and mysteries that lay beyond the grass of their yard.

Years later, when they'd grown up and had families of their own, the brothers loved to talk about the memories from their very first summer living in Virginia. The summer of the woods.

SAM LEANED his head up against the window pane and stared out into the woods of their new backyard.

Everything looked so different from their old neighborhood. It had been mostly streets and sidewalks and houses, one after the other. He could practically touch their neighbor's house while still standing in his own driveway. When he ate dinner with Derek and his parents each evening, if he looked out the window, he could often see the family next door doing the same thing. There were some trees, but just small ones that grew in front of each house.

"Nothing like these monsters," thought Sam, as he looked out into his new yard.

Mom and Dad had picked this house so the boys could have more room to play outside and be in nature. Dad had grown up on a farm in upstate New York and was tired of living in the crowded suburbs.

"Boys need room to roam," Dad had said to Mom.

"Well there's plenty of room to roam here," Sam said to himself.

"Who's going to Rome?" asked Derek as he entered the bedroom.

"No one's going to Rome, Derek," answered Sam. "That's like on the other side of the country."

"Actually, it's all the way across the Atlantic Ocean," said Derek. "Speaking of water, I want to go exploring around the creek back in the woods. It's just sitting there waiting for us. Come on, let's get some supplies and ask Mom."

The boys loaded themselves down with full explorer gear. They had hats, belts, water bottles and bandanas tied around their necks. Derek carried a dark blue backpack, which he'd packed with a couple of walkie talkies he'd received the Christmas before last. He also brought Dad's binoculars, a plastic compass, and a wilderness guidebook that showed how to build a lean-to. Ready for adventure, they ambushed their mom in the kitchen with desperate pleas to go exploring.

At first, their mom wasn't comfortable allowing the boys out in the woods very long by themselves.

"You boys don't even know what's out there," worried Mom. "Why don't you give yourselves a bit more time to get settled before I completely lose sight of you. Have you even unpacked your closet boxes yet?"

"We will, we promise," said Derek. "As soon as we get back. We really want to see the creek!"

"Mom, we need room to roam!" pleaded Sam. "Dad said so!"

Their dad heard the ruckus and came into the kitchen carrying an old stopwatch with an alarm. He tied it onto the strap of Derek's backpack.

"I set the timer for one hour," said Dad. "When the alarm goes off, it means it's time to come back home. I don't want you guys wandering too far off until you learn your way around out there. Woods like these can be great fun, but they can also be dangerous if you're not careful. Stay together so you don't get lost."

The boys agreed to his instructions and marched out the back door like they were headed off to war and ran excitedly down the hill and into the woods. As they entered the trail, it became darker beneath the canopy of trees. Huge oaks and evergreens towered above them with thick, coarse trunks that climbed high into the sky with branches and leaves only near the very top. The boys pressed on along the trail until they could hear the sound of water moving over rocks where the creek bed gurgled.

"Come on, I see it!" yelled Derek.

The creek was just a small bit of water, not a big river or even a stream. It moved slowly with occasional ripples as it passed over larger rocks, and its bed wound through the forest like a slithering snake. Old dead trees littered the woods and some lay fallen across the water, stretched out at odd angles like wooden bridges. The fallen logs were great for pirate games. Derek made Sam walk the plank over a river of ravenous crocodiles waiting to devour him.

Sam consulted his compass even though he didn't really know how to use it. He declared that they should head west – or, as Derek reminded his younger brother, they should go left. For close to an hour, the boys hopped across the small rocks that littered the water and turned over stones to hunt for salamanders and crawfish, all the while keeping a keen eye out for snakes.

The old lady who lived next door, Mrs. Haskins, had come by the day they moved in to say hi and give them a cake she had made. She warned them about Copperheads living in the woods, which Dad said were poisonous snakes. It had nearly been enough to give

Sam second thoughts about the whole exploration idea. But after some convincing by his older brother and a talk with Dad about how unlikely it was that they would see one with all the noise they made, Sam felt a little better.

"If you see a snake, just don't step on it and don't try to pick it up. Go in the other direction and leave it alone. They're more scared of you than you are of them," Dad had counseled. Sam questioned whether that was really possible, but he trusted that Dad was right.

The afternoon drew to a close and the air grew slightly cooler as the boys moved deeper through the trees. In reality they had not ventured more than a few hundred yards from where they'd begun their journey, but it seemed like miles and miles in the boys' minds. Sam walked behind his brother and pulled at the watch that hung from the backpack.

"Five more minutes left on the watch, Derek. We should start heading back."

"Okay, just a minute, I want to see what's over here," Derek answered, as he took a giant leap from the rock he'd been standing on. His foot slid across some loose dirt where he landed and he threw his arms out to keep his balance, glad not to have fallen in the water in front of his younger brother.

"Be careful, Sam," he warned, acting as if he'd crossed hundreds of much larger rivers in his life. "I'm heading up the hill to see what's over that ridge."

"I can't jump that far, Derek," yelled Sam, as he set one foot on a slippery stone and sank down to one knee in the water. A dart of color dove beneath a small stone next to his leg. He instantly thought of snakes, but he was relieved when a brightly decorated salamander jumped back out from under the rock and stood frozen in the dirt as if it thought it was camouflaged.

"Oh, you're not a snake. Where are you going, little guy?" Sam whispered quietly.

The sunlight sparkled against the iridescent blue and silver stripes that ran from its head to tail. Its tongue slipped in and out, seeming to test the air for danger. Sam reached his hand out slowly. When his fingertip bumped the salamander's tail, it leaped straight up in the air with a start and scrambled back to the creek bank and out of sight.

"Oh well," thought Sam.

He looked up for Derek but didn't see him anywhere. He began to take a step when something shiny in the water caught his eye for an instant. Sam moved over to where he'd spied the shiny object. He balanced himself on a rock and looked down into the water. At first he didn't see anything. Whatever he had seen must be very small. But when he turned his head, he saw another sparkle. He reached his hand into the creek and picked up a small round metal object that had been lying on top of a smooth stone.

"What have we here?" Sam mumbled to himself. "Whoa, a coin! Sweet!"

Sam held the coin up between his fingers and inspected it in the late afternoon sun. He saw the words *ONE CENT* in big letters across the back. It was the color of a penny, but it looked very old and not like the usual coins he'd seen.

Sam stuck the coin in his pocket and looked up.

"Derek?" he called, but he still didn't see his brother.

He peered into the woods, but he couldn't see much of anything through the thick trees. His eyes rested on a line of pines up the hill and what looked to be an enormous rock behind them.

TWO
THE BOULDER

Derek ducked through some small branches and used a stick to pull back a thorn-bush that had grabbed his shirt. He had walked up the hill towards the line of pine trees while Sam was fooling around in the water and blabbering about snakes. Derek had seen the really big rock too and discovered that it was in fact an enormous boulder. From where he stood, it was the size of a giant dump truck, and it loomed above him as he stood next to its dark shadow.

The boulder was covered with moss and leaves on small ledges that jutted here and there up its sides. Derek pulled back a group of branches along the boulder and as he did, noticed something written on the rock. He looked closer and discovered a small plaque that was laid into the side of the stone like a sign.

He leaned down and brushed it off with his hands. In large block letters was written, "Virginia Mining Company. No Trespassing."

Derek studied the plaque, surprised to see such a sign out in the middle of the woods. He wondered if he should stop but decided to keep going.

Above the plaque, ledges in the rock made something like a staircase. Derek put a foot on the nearest crevice and lifted his body up to the first ledge. He reached up for the next step when he felt something grab his ankle. He jumped and turned his head, only to find Sam peering up at him from the ground, his face in a cross expression for being abandoned at the creek.

"What are you *doing*?" Sam demanded.

"I want to see what's up here," Derek said.

"Look what I found in the creek," said Sam. He took the coin out of his pocket and showed it to Derek. "Look how the back of it is different than usual. I think it's old."

"Wow – that's pretty cool," replied Derek, studying the coin. "Check out what I found on this boulder." He reached back down and pointed at the plaque.

"Virginia Mining Company," Sam read again. "Mining, what is that, like a gold mine?"

"I doubt it," said Derek. "We'll have to ask Dad if he knows."

"I don't think we should be up here, Derek," warned Sam. "*No Trespassing* means keep out, I think."

"Nah, this is really old," said Derek. "We're fine." He proceeded to scramble up the remaining ledges towards the top.

"Wait for me!" called Sam as Derek again moved out of sight. It was a tough climb along the edges of the boulder, and there were lots of little holes that might hide a lurking snake. Nonetheless, Sam tentatively followed his brother's path up the rocks and was soon beside him.

The top of the boulder was flat and about twenty feet across. Sam looked out across the rock and realized that he could see a very long way. There was a valley ahead of them, and they were above all but the highest trees. It was a beautiful view with the drifting clouds and the deep woods all around. Derek was crouched down on his stomach at the edge of the far end of the rock.

"Get down!" he said, and waved his hand at Sam to move back.

"What is it?"

"Shhhh!" Derek hissed. He reached into his backpack and retrieved the binoculars.

As Derek fumbled with the binocular dials, Sam stretched his neck over the side. He looked down below the boulder and realized that it was much farther down on this side of the rock than the side they'd climbed up. It was a cliff, maybe fifty feet to the bottom, and would certainly be way too steep to go all the way down. He instinctively scooted back a few inches on the rock so that he wasn't so close to the edge.

"Whoa," whispered Derek slowly. "Look at that."

"Let me see," said Sam. "What is it?"

Derek didn't answer and stayed perched on his elbows, staring through the binoculars.

"Let me see!" he repeated, and yanked the binoculars from Derek's hands.

"Hey!" said Derek, but Sam already had the binoculars to his eyes and pointed down the cliff. He was just about to ask his brother what the big deal was, when he heard a noise below him. He moved his binoculars towards the sound, but he only saw branches. Then, behind the branch, he caught a faint glimpse of something black moving.

"What was *that*?" Sam whispered.

"I don't know because you took the binoculars," complained Derek. "Give those to me!" He snatched them back.

Sam looked back down and saw two boys walking around at the base of the rocks. They looked to be about the same age as he and Derek, maybe a little bit older. They were doing some kind of work around the bottom of the boulder. One pushed a wheelbarrow full of branches, pieces of wood and other stuff. He took it away from the boulder to a spot just a few feet into the trees where it appeared that there was a small structure.

Maybe it's a fort, thought Sam. He looked back at the other boy who was still near the boulder. He could see him for a few seconds, but then he disappeared out of sight, only to reappear again. There must be some kind of crevice or cave down there.

"Who is that, Derek?"

"Shhh! I don't know. Be still, I want to move a little closer to see what they're doing."

"I think we should get out of here, Derek. Where are you going to go?"

But Derek didn't answer. He had already begun to hang his left foot over the edge of the rock and was carefully climbing down at an angle to the next ledge where there was a bush that he could hide behind.

As he found his footing and brought his other leg down, the silence was suddenly interrupted by a loud "BEEP! BEEP! BEEP!" The alarm was sounding from the stopwatch hanging from the strap on his backpack!

Startled, Derek lost his balance and slipped a couple feet down the slope of the rock, until his fall was stopped roughly by the bush. A cascade of loose gravel scattered ahead of him down the rock face, and his arm banged hard against the edge of the boulder as he fell. A sharp pain ran through his body.

"Derek!" Sam yelled. He stood up to see where his brother had fallen.

At the sound of Sam's yell and the watch beeping, the activity at the bottom of the hill stopped, and the other boys turned their heads up towards the peak of the boulder. Derek frantically pressed buttons on the watch to end the beeping, but it wouldn't stop. He gave up and turned to climb, but as he stood up from behind the bush, he came into full view of the boys below.

"Hey you!" one of the boys shouted. The shout was accompanied by a terrible sounding growl and a huge blur of black fur that Derek only caught a glimpse of.

"Bear! Get back here!" the boy shouted and ran towards the side of the boulder and out of sight.

The black blur had also vanished, but Derek heard a loud growling that seemed to be getting closer. He quickly made his way back up to where Sam was standing, and the two of them ran up to the front of the boulder.

"Come on!" Derek called to his brother as he scampered down the rocks. Sam just stood there frozen with bulging eyes, thinking that the new boys or a bear were going to emerge from around the rock any second.

"Sam! Run!" Derek yelled again. He reached up and tugged his brother's arm, practically pulling him down the rock staircase.

They tore around the line of trees and down the slope to the creek as fast as they could without tripping over branches and stones. The shouts of their pursuers echoed in the distance, but they didn't dare turn around and look. Instead, they splashed right into the creek, not worrying about finding a stone to leap across, and soaking their sneakers and clothes. Sam didn't have time to think about snakes.

"Stop!" they heard behind them.

But by now the brothers were stomping through the undergrowth and moving back east along the creek towards home. Sharp branches and leaves smacked them in the face and arms as they hurtled through the brush. Derek could feel his elbow burning from where he banged it against the rock, and Sam had a cramp in his side that made him feel like he was going to throw up.

But they didn't stop. They just kept running.

As they neared the part of the creek that ran behind their house, Derek realized that he couldn't hear growling or yelling any more. He saw the spot where the trees parted and the green grass of their backyard began. They charged up the slope and around to the cover of their front yard.

As they jumped up the porch steps, their mom opened the door. The two boys nearly knocked her over as they came spilling through the threshold, dirty and dripping wet. They started babbling about attackers and bears and nearly being killed, but they weren't making much sense. Mom saw blood on Derek's elbow, and she ordered them both out onto the deck to take off their wet shoes and clothes while she got some disinfectant and a bandage for his arm.

Out of breath, the boys didn't have the strength to argue, so they headed out the back door onto the elevated deck. Neither spoke as they sat and removed the muddy shoes that clung to their wet socks like suction cups. Both just stared off into the distance, replaying in their minds what had just happened. They were too astonished to know what to say, their hearts still beating fast in their chests.

Sam picked up his shoes and walked over to the railing. He pulled off his wet shirt and hung it over the wood. He felt in his pocket for the coin he had found in the creek and was glad to see that it was still there.

Derek looked down over the yard to where the trail began in the woods and gasped.

Sam saw his brother's pale face. "What's wrong?"

Derek didn't answer, but when Sam followed his brother's stare to the woods, his heart sank. Under the branches a few feet into the tree line loomed a dark shadow and a pair of eyes peering out from the trees.

"Okay, come over here, you two. I found the box with the first aid kit!" Mom announced triumphantly.

Her voice startled them as she opened the back door and walked out on the deck with the antiseptic and bandages in hand. Both boys nearly jumped out of their skin.

"Mom! Shhh!" they shrieked and ducked down behind the railing.

"What?" Mom asked, surprised at their panic as she walked over.

"Look!" whispered Sam as he peered out from behind his wet shirt hanging on the railing.

"Look at what?" asked Mom.

"By the woods, over there," said Sam, pointing towards the trail. But when he peeked up and looked out at the woods to show her, there was nothing there.

THREE

THE COIN

After the chase through the woods, Derek and Sam decided to stay indoors for a little while. Not that they were scared, they just wanted to take a break.

Okay, admitted Sam, that first night in bed after the lights had gone out, maybe he was a little scared. When he closed his eyes in the dark, he could still feel himself running back home with the leaves and branches all a blur around them.

Derek had tried to describe what had happened to Dad earlier that night, but when he talked about it, the words didn't come out right. It sounded to Dad like they had played a game of tag or something in the woods with some friends.

"Why don't you just stay away from that part of the

woods for a while," Dad had counseled. That seemed like a good idea to Sam.

After breakfast, Sam went up to his room and pulled the coin he'd found in the creek from his desk drawer. It was dark colored but clean from the water. He held the old coin up under the light.

On the front, it looked like a regular penny. Abraham Lincoln's picture was in the middle. Honest Abe, he'd heard him called. Along the top edge, he could just barely make out the words *In God We Trust*. Sam thought he remembered seeing that on a lot of coins, so that part wasn't different.

To the left of Honest Abe was the word *Liberty*. He'd heard that word in the Pledge of Allegiance in the mornings at school but wasn't really sure what it meant. He'd ask Derek.

The last thing he noticed on the front of the coin was a date. 1931. That seemed pretty old. Maybe even older than Dad! Sam would have to ask Dad when he was born, he couldn't remember.

He turned the coin over and saw what had gotten his attention in the woods. This part looked different than the pennies he'd seen before. *ONE CENT* was written across the middle of the coin, and underneath in smaller letters it said, *United States of America*. Some odd-looking markings were along the sides and at the top were some tiny letters that he couldn't make any sense of.

He shook a newer penny out of his piggy bank and inspected it. The back had a picture of a building. He was pretty sure it was the Lincoln Memorial in Washington, DC. They'd visited it on one of their house-hunting trips to Virginia that spring. That made sense, thought Sam, since Abraham Lincoln was on the front.

Sam went back to those words that he couldn't understand. He noticed it was on the newer penny as well. He tried to read what they said, but the letters were small and rubbed worn. "E....Pluri...bus....U...num. I wonder what that means?" he said aloud.

"What what means?" asked Derek as he walked into the bedroom. "What are you looking at?"

Sam jumped at Derek's voice. He was always sneaking up and surprising him.

"I'm trying to read the words on this old coin. It has strange letters on it that I don't understand. Look, it's on this new penny too."

"It looks like a different language," said Derek. "Let's ask Dad if he knows what it is."

Sam picked up both the coins and they headed downstairs. Their dad was working in his office, next to the living room.

"Dad, we need your help!" called Derek as they

reached the bottom of the stairs and bounded into his office. He was filling up an empty shelf with books from a box next to the desk.

"We have this old coin and can't read what it says. It looks like Chinese or something!" exclaimed Sam.

"Chinese? Well that seems unlikely," smiled Dad, as he set down a book. "Let's see what you have here." Sam handed him the old and the new coins.

"Look, I think these are both pennies, but this one is really old. It says it's from 1931. Is that when you were born?"

"1931?" laughed Dad, making a face like he was insulted. "No Sam, I'm not that old, thank you very much. 1931 is ten years before Grandpa was born. You'll have to ask *him* if that's old or not and see what he says! Where are those words you couldn't read?"

"Right here," replied Sam, and he flipped the coin over and showed his dad the small letters. "It says '*A Power Bus Oven*' or something crazy like that."

Dad squinted at the coin. "I may not have been born in 1931, but that is still some very small print. Let me get my magnifying glass." He walked over to the closet and pulled a box off the shelf.

"Here we go," he said and sat down at his desk with the magnifying glass and leaned forward under the light. "*E Pluribus Unum.* That's Latin, boys. It means "Out of Many, One."

"Out of Many, One," repeated Sam. "What in the world does that mean? Why would they put that on a coin?"

"Maybe it means that many coins should come to one person, like me, so I can be rich!" suggested Derek.

"I don't think so, Derek," laughed Dad. "I think it has something to do with our country being made of different parts but yet still all the same nation. I'm sure you'll learn about it in history class soon.

"But look here," continued Dad, "I see that this is a wheat penny."

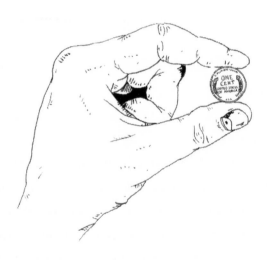

"A wheat penny? What is a wheat penny?" asked Sam.

"Is it made of wheat?" asked Derek. "Here, let me eat it, I'm hungry!"

"No, Derek," said Dad. "It's a bit hard to see on this one because it's so old, but if you look carefully under my magnifying glass, you can see two stalks of wheat along the sides of the coin. That's why they call it a wheat penny. Here, let me find a picture of one on the Internet so you can better see what it looks like."

Dad did a quick Google search for "wheat penny" on his laptop and pulled up a screen full of coins that looked much shinier than the one he held in his hand. He clicked on one of the pictures to make it bigger. Just as he had described, there were two stalks of wheat, one on each side of the coin.

"So that's why they call it a wheat penny," said Sam. "Pretty cool."

"How much is it worth?" asked Derek. "Five million dollars?"

"Probably not," said Dad, "but let's see." He clicked on a link to coin values and scrolled down until he came to the year 1931. "If this was in perfect – or what's called mint condition, it could be worth up to five dollars. Do you think this is in perfect shape like the ones on the computer?"

"No, this one is pretty old and worn," moaned Derek. "How much is that worth?"

"Well," said Dad, "it looks like ours is worth about thirty-five cents, which is not so bad when you consider that it used to be worth only one cent. Wow, look here, it says that there were several different kinds of pennies over the years. Wheat pennies were minted, which means made, between 1909 to 1956, when they changed to the Lincoln penny that we have today."

"It has the Lincoln Memorial building on the back," added Sam.

"That's right, very good, Sam," said Dad.

"What came before the wheat penny, Dad?" asked Derek.

"Let's see," said Dad. "Before the wheat penny was the Indian Head cent from 1859 to 1909."

"Does that one have an Indian on the front?" asked Derek.

"Actually," said Dad, scrolling through the page on the computer screen, "it says here that the coin doesn't actually have a picture of an Indian, or what we call a Native American, but a picture of Lady Liberty wearing a feather headdress."

"Lady Liberty?" said Sam. "Who in the world is that? Benjamin Franklin's girlfriend? This is getting confusing."

"Are they valuable?" asked Derek.

"Not all of them," answered Dad, "it depends on the year and their condition. Some can be worth just a couple of dollars. But here, look at this one – the 1877 Indian Head cent is one of the rarest coins and can be worth up to $5,000."

"Wow!" shouted Sam. "That's a lot of money! Do you have any Indian Head cents?"

"No," said Dad, "I don't think we have any of those. I'd guess only coin collectors and museums would have a coin like that."

Just then Dad's phone rang. "I have to answer this, boys. We can talk more about this later."

Sam picked up the coins and the boys walked into the hallway. "Those pennies are cool. I wonder why the wheat penny was out there in the woods. Do you think there's any more?"

"I don't know," replied Derek, "but I want an Indian Head cent."

"I'd go back and look," said Sam, "but it was over by that boulder and those kids and the bear! I don't want to run into them again."

"I've been thinking about that," said Derek. "It couldn't have been a bear. Why would those kids have been playing so close to a bear?"

"No, they yelled 'bear!' I heard them," declared

Sam. "I don't know why, but I heard them say it. And there was definitely an animal chasing us. I'm not going back."

"We'll see," said Derek as the doorbell rang.

The boys walked up to the glass next to the front door and saw Mr. Haskins, their neighbor, standing outside. Derek opened the door.

"Hello, Mr. Haskins."

"Hi, boys," Mr. Haskins answered in a crusty old voice. "I've got some of your mail that the post office put in my box by mistake."

He took a couple of envelopes out of his jacket. It was the middle of summer, but for some reason, old people seemed to always dress like it was winter, noticed Sam. He thought Mr. Haskins must be a hundred years old.

"Were you born in 1931?" Sam blurted out before he could think better of it. Mr. Haskins was old, maybe he knew about the coins.

"1931!" Mr. Haskins grinned. "No, I was born in 1935. Born right in that house you see there in front of you." He gestured over his shoulder at his house. It seemed even older than theirs. "We didn't need fancy hospitals like you kids are born in today. Come to think of it, my older brother, Harold Haskins, was born in 1931, but he died when he was only eight."

He leaned in close to the boys and looked them right in the eye. Sam wished he hadn't talked to the old man. Mr. Haskins was creepy.

"Died right there in those woods behind your house. Fell in a hole." Mr. Haskins paused a moment like he was going to say more about the holes but didn't. He looked at Sam and said in an eerie voice, "How old are you, son?"

Sam gulped. "Eight," he whispered, and felt a shiver go down his spine. He was so nervous that he dropped the penny out of his hand and bent down to pick it up.

"Hey, what ya got there?" asked Mr. Haskins. "Have a coin, do ya? Let me see that."

Sam handed him the coin. Derek looked over his shoulder towards Dad's office for some assistance, but he was still on the phone, gesturing with his hands and looking down at some papers.

Mr. Haskins held the coin up. "Well I'll be! I haven't seen one of these for a while. You've got yourself a wheat penny. Where'd you find that, boy?"

"In the woods," Sam muttered and looked down at his shoes. He saw his lace was untied. He wondered if Mr. Haskins would notice if he wandered off to tie it and didn't come back. He was sorry that he'd brought up 1931 in the first place.

"He found it in the creek yesterday," said Derek, trying to help his younger brother.

"Must'a been thirty years since I held one of these," Mr. Haskins continued, still looking at the old coin. "I wonder if this came from the...nah, couldn't have been."

"Came from what?" asked Sam. He was now suddenly more interested in Mr. Haskins than his shoe.

"Oh, back when I was a teenager, there was a big excitement around these parts when someone broke into the Virginia Museum and stole a collection of rare coins. It was all over the newspapers. The coppers interviewed a whole bunch of people, including the family that lived in this house of yours – Davis was their name, I think. Seems the man who lived here worked as a security guard at the museum and they suspected that he might be involved.

"Richard Davis, that was his name. Odd fella. He'd been in prison or something suspicious like that. But they never could prove that he took the coins and eventually the police gave up. Most folks 'round here forgot about it and got on with their normal business."

"What happened to the coins?" asked Derek.

"Never found 'em. Oh, every once in a while, some yahoo would claim they found them and haul in a whole bunch of old coins, but they weren't worth much and weren't the museum coins."

"Hello, Jonas." The boys jumped and turned around as their dad approached behind them.

"Hi, Bill. Brought some of your mail that the daggone postman delivered to me by mistake. Lived here over eighty years and they still can't give me the right mail. I tell you what!" Mr. Haskins complained. "I was just giving your boys some local history lessons."

He turned to leave but looked back at Sam. "Good luck with your wheat penny, son. You stay out of trouble now. And watch out for them holes," he said in that creepy voice again and smiled.

Sam gulped and watched him slowly walk away.

FOUR
THE STORM

That night, there was a big storm. Derek woke up to a crash so loud that he thought the ground had been hit by a wrecking ball. The whole house shook and rattled. He pulled his covers up over his nose, leaving just enough space so his eyes could peek out.

Lightning flashed through the bedroom windows like a spotlight. For a moment he could see everything in his room like it was the middle of the day. But then the light vanished and he was surrounded by darkness again.

BOOM! Another thunderbolt clapped down as if the huge trees in the woods were tumbling to the ground. It was the angels in heaven at the bowling alley, Mom had told him.

Derek leaned carefully over the railing of his bunk bed and looked down at the bed below.

"Sam!"

No answer.

A flash of lightning illuminated the room once more and Derek saw his brother's face peacefully sleeping beneath him. Sam could sleep through anything. He never woke up during thunderstorms. Derek figured they could have an earthquake or even an alien invasion and Sam wouldn't know the difference. It was crazy. Derek woke up at the slightest noise. It just wasn't fair.

He hated thunderstorms. He always had, and even though he was older now and knew that nothing bad was going to happen, he still hated everything about them. The rain, the wind, the lightning, the thunder – all of it. Dad joked that he should be a weatherman. A meteorologist, he had called it – a type of scientist that studies the weather. Definitely not, Derek had responded.

Another flash and crash filled the sky. The rain pounded against the skylight on the roof outside his room and sounded like someone spilling bags of pebbles on the glass over and over again. It was so loud!

Derek sat up in bed, too nervous to go back to sleep. He climbed down the bunk bed ladder and crept along the dark hallway toward his parents' bedroom. Usually, the creaks and groans of the house's old wood floorboards would have alerted them of his arrival, but the rain and the storm were so loud that Derek couldn't even hear his *own* footsteps.

He inched forward, feeling the wall for guidance towards his parents' doorway. His foot bumped something hard and he lost his balance. Lightning flashed and he watched himself awkwardly tumble down into a laundry basket filled with folded underwear and socks. Thud!

Derek lay in the basket. If it had been daytime, he would have been embarrassed to be lying in the pile of underwear, but he was still half asleep. It was actually kind of cozy. Maybe he would just stay here until the storm was over. Why was he up wandering around in the middle of the night anyway? It was just a stupid storm. Sam didn't seem to mind, and he was younger than Derek.

The thunder crashed loud again, and he instinctively reached his hands up to pull himself out of the basket and flee to his parents' room. But when his leg stretched out of the basket, it smacked into the bottom part of the wall along the floor with a strange hollow thud.

"Oh great," groaned Derek, thinking he had kicked a hole in the wall.

The house was old, and some parts already needed fixing. He bent over and pushed on the white trim board along the floor with his hands. To his surprise, it moved in slightly.

"That's strange," thought Derek.

He pushed again, a little harder this time. The board moved forward and then swung out a few inches towards him from one side, as if on a hinge, revealing a small opening in the wall.

"Whoa," whispered Derek, no longer thinking about the thunder and lightning. He stood up, slid the laundry basket away and reached his arm into the wall, pushing his shoulder against the floor. His hand inched forward into the opening, feeling around the floor and the wall beams.

The hidden space didn't seem very large, but it was hard for Derek to tell in the dark. He could feel a thick layer of dirt and dust on everything he touched, and he hoped that there weren't any mice or bugs lurking in the corners.

When another flash of lightning filled the house with light, he saw something. At least he thought he did. A box was on the far side of the compartment. As quickly as he saw it, there was blackness again when the lightning faded and darkness overtook the house.

Derek stretched his arm as far as it could go into the hole. His fingertips brushed the edge of the box. He strained his arm some more, pushing his shoulder and armpit into the wall so hard that they started to sting. His fingers reached around the edge of the box and tugged it slightly toward him, moving it an inch. And then another inch. Soon he was able to put his hand around it, and he pulled the box out of the hole.

Derek pushed the board back into place in the wall and held the small wooden box in his hands. He leaned against the wall in the darkness, thinking. His heart fluttered, and his mind raced with his discovery. Why would there be a secret compartment in the wall of the house? Who in the world would have put it there? Most importantly, what was in this mystery box?

It was too dark in the hallway to see, so as quietly as he could, Derek tiptoed over to the stairs and down to the kitchen for a flashlight. He brought it over to the couch in the family room and set the box on the coffee table. As he shined his light on the box, he could see that it was old, not too large - about the size of a small shoebox - and it was covered with dust, just like the hole had been. A small metal clasp on the front held the lid shut, and on the top he could see some faint letters engraved into the wood. Derek brushed the dust off with his hand and studied the carving.

"VMC," he read. What did that mean? It seemed familiar, but he couldn't place it.

Derek's fingers moved back to the clasp, which he found moved easily. His head was feeling dizzy and he realized he'd been holding his breath with excitement. He closed his eyes for a moment, took a deep breath, and slowly opened the box.

When he opened his eyes, Derek saw an old piece of yellow paper folded up into a square. He picked it up and carefully unfolded it. It was a newspaper clipping from the *Virginia Times*.

He looked for a date along the top – August 8,

1953. The headline read, "Valuable Coins Stolen from Virginia Museum."

He placed the paper down on the table and looked back in the box. He pulled out a small notebook. It had a thin leather cover with the same "VMC" letters on the front that were carved into the box.

"VMC," he thought to himself again. Where did he know that from? Then it hit him – the plaque by the boulder in the woods. VMC – Virginia Mining Company! Could that be it? But why would there be a box and book from the Virginia Mining Company hidden in the wall of the house? This was getting interesting.

Written in pencil on the inside cover of the notebook was, "R. Davis." Richard Davis was the name of the man that Mr. Haskins said used to live in this house and was questioned by the police, thought Derek. Was this his notebook?

He flipped through more pages but it seemed to just be facts and figures about supplies, operations, and other stuff that he didn't really understand. He was about to close the notebook when something caught his eye. Near the end was a series of drawings. They looked like rough depictions of mine passageways and caverns. But what interested him most was the drawing on the last page – a simple sketch of a coin.

Derek leaned in and looked closely at the drawing. He quickly recognized the feathered headdress of Lady Liberty on the Indian Head cent. He flipped back and studied the drawings again and realized what he was looking at. It was a map! A map of a mine tunnel and a picture of an Indian Head cent.

Derek looked back into the box. It seemed empty except for a pile of dirt in the corner. His finger pushed at the dust only to feel something move. It was hard and round. A coin? His eyes opened wide in the dark room as he blew the dust off the coin and shined his light on it. He blinked through the dust as he read the words *ONE CENT* across the back. He flipped it over and looked into the face of a woman wearing a feathered hat.

"No way!" thought Derek. He was holding an Indian Head cent just like Dad had described to them earlier! *1895*, it read along the bottom. Not 1877, he thought, disappointed, but still pretty old.

He placed the coin back in the box and read the newspaper clipping.

Yesterday, at the Virginia Museum, a prominent display of mid-nineteenth century coins was brazenly stolen from the Thomas C. Pendergass gallery. Police reported that the crime took place sometime between the hours of its 6 PM closing and the first tour the following day.

"It is a tragedy that this beautiful collection would be stolen," said museum curator William Evanshade, Jr. "Not strictly for its monetary value, but also because of its important place in the history of American currency."

Authorities have reportedly held several museum employees for questioning, including one Richard Davis, a security guard. Davis has a previously unknown criminal record, including charges of burglary.

The clock on the mantel suddenly chimed, and Derek jumped and looked up from the newspaper. He flashed his light toward it and saw the hands pointing to two o'clock. He realized that he was very tired and leaned back into the couch and started reading some more from the newspaper. But before long, his eyes were closed and he was sound asleep.

FIVE
THE CREEK

Derek pulled his hand over his face. Sunlight streamed through the window and the room glowed in the early morning light. He sat up. The rain had stopped. He looked around and realized he was in the family room. It took him a minute to remember how he'd arrived there during the storm.

He looked down and saw the old newspaper clipping lying on the floor. He folded it back up and placed it in the box. The excitement of his discovery was still a bit cloudy from his short night of sleep, and he wasn't quite sure what to do next. He gathered the box and its contents and quietly walked back upstairs. He tried not to wake anyone with the creaks in the floors, which could now be clearly heard in the quiet of the morning.

He wandered down the hall to his bedroom where Sam still lay comatose.

Derek leaned over the bed and stared into Sam's sleeping face. He was so close that their eyes were just inches apart. He stood there motionless for a few moments, his head frozen above the bed like a spider lurking above its prey. Sam didn't move a muscle. Derek gave a little tickle to Sam's arm through the sheets, but he still didn't move. Growing impatient, Derek decided to speed the process up a bit and gave his brother a hard poke in the ribs with his finger.

"Ahhh!" cried Sam as his whole body jumped and his eyes opened. He was surprised to see two eyeballs looking back at him. He tried to sit up but instead he conked his forehead right into his older brother's nose.

"Ow!" cried Derek.

"Ow!" said Sam. "What are you doing?"

"It stopped raining," answered Derek. "Let's go outside before Mom and Dad wake up."

Sam just moaned, rubbed his head and turned over in his bed. "What rain?" he said. "I'm tired."

"There was a huge storm last night," replied Derek. "Not that you'd know, since you slept through it as always."

"Really?"

"Really. Let's go! Get dressed. I want to get back to

the creek. And you are not going to believe what I found."

He held the box out in front of Sam and explained how he'd discovered it in the night and what was inside. Sam's jaw dropped open as Derek held up the Indian Head cent.

"No way!" Sam exclaimed. He took it from Derek and held it up carefully. "We have to show this to Dad!"

"Not yet," said Derek. "I want to try to figure this mystery out on our own first. If we find the stolen coins, we could be heroes!"

Derek pulled his desk chair over to the closet. He lifted the old box high over his head until it slid onto the top shelf, and he threw an old sweatshirt overtop of it.

"For safe keeping," he explained. "If it's been hidden for all these years, a little while longer won't hurt anything, Sam. Come on, let's go to the creek!"

* * *

THE TWO BOYS raced silently across the backyard and down the path to the creek. Both of their minds were too consumed with the thoughts of Derek's discovery to talk. Their sneakers quickly became wet from the grass, as the storm had left everything soaked.

Even though the sun was up, the air was still and quiet, except for the occasional cry of a red-tailed hawk that circled high above the trees.

The boys had seen the creek a few times now since moving in, but they could tell that things were different even before they reached it. The sound of rushing water called out through the otherwise quiet forest. When they arrived at the water's edge, the boys slowly climbed up one of the fallen log bridges, putting one foot in front of another, careful not to step on the wet, slippery mosses along the edges. They maneuvered to a spot that gave them a clear view of the water.

The storm had turned the lazy flow of water into a surging stream that moved through the twists and turns of the creek bed with a newfound force. The water had risen at least two feet higher and wider onto the soft banks of sand and dirt where the boys usually stood to throw stones. Piles of leaves and branches had been pushed onto the dirt overtop of the normal walking trails. In fact, the large sticks that they had used as bridges over muddy spots on the ground had been completely washed away and were piled up with the other debris that was caught in the bends of the creek.

Sam suddenly stopped thinking about Derek's discovery of the box and marveled at the creek. "What happened?" he asked.

"There was a lot of rain last night," answered Derek. "I told you the storm was big even though you didn't hear it."

"Yeah, you weren't kidding," said Sam.

The boys stepped off the log and slowly found their way to the edge of the bank, following the creek farther into the woods. Sam agreed to go toward the area where he'd found the coin, as long as they didn't go up near the boulder.

The boys had a tough time seeing along the bottom of the creek, since the water was so high and fast-moving from the storm. The stones looked blurry beneath the current, which was like the white water streaking from the jets in a hot tub.

"It seems like if there was one wheat penny in here, there might be others," reasoned Derek as they walked up and down the creek bank peering into the water.

"Why would there be old pennies in the creek at all?" wondered Sam.

Derek looked up at Sam. "Don't you remember what Mr. Haskins said about that museum robbery? He said that the man they tried to arrest used to live in our house, Richard Davis."

"You believe him?" asked Sam. "I think he's crazy. He spooks me out with all that talk of his brother falling into a hole and dying."

"I don't know about his brother, but the museum robbery was real. It was in the newspaper article in the box. Plus, the notebook had *R. Davis* written in the cover, the map of the passageways, and it had a real Indian Head cent. It all points to one thing!"

"What?" said Sam. "What does it point to?"

"Do I have to spell it out for you, Sam? The treasure, it's out here. Somewhere by the boulder and that Virginia Mining Company sign. It has to be. And I'm going to find it!"

"Hmm," said Sam. "How do you know it's by the

boulder? Maybe he really did steal them but then threw them here in the creek!"

"He wouldn't throw a valuable coin collection in the creek, Sam. That wouldn't make any sense. Would you throw money in a creek?"

"I've thrown pennies in the fountain at the mall," answered Sam. "Maybe the police were hot on his trail."

"Just forget it," sighed Derek in frustration. "This a stupid conversation and a waste of time. There's nothing here and we'd never find anything with all this fast-moving water. Let's head home."

"Wait a minute, Derek," said Sam. "I just want to look more downstream from where I found the penny."

Sam walked slowly along the edge of the creek bed slope, eyes fixed down in the water. He came to a spot where the trees overhead parted in the sky, allowing the sunlight to stream down into the water.

Suddenly Sam spied something glimmering in the light. He got down on his knees and bent lower to see what it was.

"Derek, look, do you see that?"

"Where?"

"Right there, next to that square-shaped rock sticking out of the water. See those spots sparkling in the sunlight? Are those coins?"

"I don't know, they're kind of small, it's hard to tell," answered Derek.

"Let me see if I can move one with a stick so we can tell if it's a coin," said Sam.

He picked out a long stick from the brush and leaned further over the bank, stretching his arm as far as he could toward the sparkle. The edge of the stick pushed into the wet dirt around the shiny object and then lightly touched it.

"Look at that!" yelled Sam, "something moved and it was round! I'm telling you, they're coins – just like I found before. I have to get them! Here, hold my legs. This branch isn't long enough, and I need to reach down there."

Derek sat down on the ground behind him and held onto his brother's dangling feet. "Sam, be careful. You're not going to be able to reach them, it's too far down. Let's go around to the other side."

"No, this is better," Sam yelled up as he looked into the water. "Yep, they're coins! I can see them. Sweet! There's a few – one, two, three…"

As Sam said *three*, the stick that he was balancing on split in two with a loud SNAP! He lost his balance and went sliding forward down the edge of the bank. His fingers scratched at the dirt as he slid, but there was nothing to hold on to.

Sam's sudden burst forward sent Derek falling backward and left him holding only an empty sneaker. He watched his brother slide head-first out of his view and over the edge of the creek bank.

"Sam!"

Derek pushed himself off the ground and ran to the edge of the creek. He looked down and saw Sam's body lying in the water on a rock as the current streamed by. His head was above water, but it was turned the other way and Derek couldn't see his face to tell if he was okay.

"Sam!" he called out again, but there was no answer.

Derek looked for a way to get down to him without falling too. He began to panic. He looked back at Sam but his brother still hadn't moved. He looked up the bank a few yards and saw a small sapling tree growing right up the side of the creek bank. It leaned out over the water in a curve like a backwards letter 'C'.

Derek didn't think any longer, he just wrapped his arm around the thin tree limb and dangled himself out over the water. He counted to three and let go. Those five feet that he fell into the creek seemed like twenty as he splashed down into the water. His feet slipped on the rounded rocks and the water came up to his waist. He ran, slipped and paddled his way towards Sam.

Derek reached out and pulled at Sam's wet shirt. He lifted him up and slowly turned his head over. Sam's eyes were closed and his face was splattered with mud. Derek couldn't tell if he was breathing. His mind raced with thoughts of what to do.

"Help!" Derek screamed out. "Somebody help!"

He knew that you were supposed to do CPR or mouth-to-mouth something, but he wasn't sure exactly how it worked. His teachers had said they were going to learn about it next year in gym class, but he needed to know now!

Derek leaned over and opened Sam's mouth with his fingers. He pushed his lips over his brother's mouth and started to blow. He felt Sam's face move. Then it smiled. Derek looked up and saw a mischievous glimmer in his eyes, and then Sam started to laugh.

"Got you, Derek!" yelled Sam, as he sat up in the water.

"Sam! Are you crazy? I thought you were dead!" screamed Derek.

"You love me, you really love me!" giggled Sam, and he splashed Derek with his hand in the water.

"I'm going to kill you!" yelled Derek, and he pushed his brother under the water.

Sam bounced back up. "The water actually feels pretty good! And look!" He brought his hand out from under the water and revealed several coins. "I grabbed them when I fell down the bank. I told you they were coins!"

Derek rolled his eyes. "You're unbelievable." He waded up to the spot in the creek where the coins had been, pushing his brother down into the water again with a splash as he went.

The boys climbed back to dry land and spread the coins out on a smooth spot in the dirt. There were five coins in all – another wheat penny, an unusual looking nickel with a buffalo on the back from 1932, and three silver coins from the 1920s that were the size of dimes but had a lady's head on the front with wings coming out of the sides.

"No Indian Head cents," moaned Derek, disappointed. But these coins were still pretty cool. It was even more fun than opening packs of baseball cards. "These are pretty worn from being in the water, but I bet they're still worth something."

"They keep getting weirder and weirder," marveled Sam, holding up the one with wings on it. "I wonder what these others are called. We'll have to look online like Dad did before. He's going to be surprised!"

"No, I still don't want to tell him about all of this yet," decided Derek. "I want to figure out where that map leads. I think there's a bigger treasure out here.

These are all just smaller clues. This wouldn't have been enough to steal from a museum. The treasure has got to be near that boulder, but I'm afraid that Dad will say it's too dangerous."

"But it *is* too dangerous," argued Sam. "Let's see – there's a cliff, those crazy kids, oh, and a bear! Do you want to get attacked by a bear? I'm telling Dad."

Derek grabbed Sam's arm and looked him in the eye. "Don't tell Dad," he warned slowly. "It's not dangerous. You saw those other kids playing down there, how bad could it be? Besides, it's a treasure, Sam. How often do kids our age get to hunt for a real-life treasure?"

Sam looked at the coins on the ground and thought about the treasure. "Do you really think these coins could be clues to a treasure?"

"Definitely," Derek answered confidently. "Look at all these coins. It has to be connected. You have to trust me, Sam."

"Okay," said Sam slowly, still a little uncertain, "but I'm coming with you."

SIX

THE FOURTH OF JULY

July hit Virginia that summer like a furnace. The temperature rose higher and higher, eclipsing one hundred degrees. The ancient air conditioning system in the boys' house groaned from constant use, and the grass around the yard was slowly turning a crispy brown. It was too hot to play outside, so Sam and Derek spent hours plotting out their search for the missing treasure.

Derek doubted that anyone else knew about the coins, since there surely couldn't be another map like the one he'd found in the box. But who knows, those other kids could stumble upon it by accident any day, and then it would be gone. He was determined to get there first, but they hadn't been able to find a good time to sneak out.

The next day was the Fourth of July, and despite their protests to Mom and Dad that they had much more important things to do, the boys dragged themselves into the minivan. Mom assured them that there would be lots of fun things to do when they reached the park for a holiday cookout and fireworks with their aunt and uncle and cousins.

"But Mom, we really don't have time for this today," argued Derek.

"Yeah, we have a lot to do," added Sam. "Very important things!"

"What could you have to do that's more important than our nation's birthday?" asked Mom. "How would you like it if we skipped your birthday? Did you know that a lot of important historical events happened right here in Virginia? I'm sure you'll learn about many of them in school this year."

"Is this where Lady Liberty lived?" giggled Derek.

"No, but there was a famous speech about liberty delivered by someone named Patrick Henry right here in Richmond," answered Mom.

"Did he say *Liberty and Justice for All?*" asked Sam.

"No, that was Superman," said Derek.

Mom laughed. "No, wise-guys. Patrick Henry said, 'Give me liberty or give me death.'"

"Whoa, that's serious," said Derek. "He must have really loved her."

Sam gave Derek a strange look.

"What?"

"You know, Lady Liberty. That Henry Ford guy must have really loved her if he would rather die than live without her," explained Derek.

"Oh brother," moaned Sam.

"Patrick Henry," corrected Mom. "And liberty is not a she – it's a thing. It means freedom. Which is why we think about it on the Fourth of July, when America declared its independence, or freedom, from England. Patrick Henry argued that Virginia should join the revolution, and they did."

"Was it a New Year's revolution?" asked Derek. "Those are really hard to keep."

Sam looked at his brother again. "Seriously, Derek?" Derek just laughed.

"Here we are!" shouted Dad as they turned into the state park and pulled up next to their uncle's big pickup truck. Everyone piled out and brought all their food and supplies over to picnic tables under a pavilion for a tasty meal of burgers, hot dogs, and corn on the cob.

A little while after the meal, everyone swam out to the middle of the nearby pond and enjoyed the cool water. Sam and Derek's aunt and uncle had a pair of

Retrievers that came along to cool off from the heat, and the two dogs ran and jumped in the water like they were born to swim. The boys threw a tennis ball to each other in the shallow areas, and the dogs jumped back and forth, trying to grab every throw out of the air.

An old wooden platform floated off the far shore of the pond. The kids jumped in and out of the water, judging each other's best cannonball splash. Uncle Drew said that the water was nearly twenty feet deep. When no one was looking, Derek gathered up his courage and did his very best dive into the water. At first, he was scared, but as he got deeper down, he loved how the water grew ice cold where the sun did not reach. It felt like he'd escaped from the heat into some unknown glacial waters.

Derek stayed down as long as he could in the cold water. When it felt as if his lungs would burst, he kicked and pulled with all his strength back up to the surface. When his head broke through, he sucked in the warm air and smiled at the fun.

After everyone had their fill of swimming, the families all dried off and walked over to the other side of the park where the locals gathered for the fireworks celebration. Camp chairs were unfolded and set up in a row. A big blanket was spread out in the grass for the younger cousins to sit on.

Derek stared up and watched the last pieces of sunlight slip from the western horizon as the sky faded into darkness.

"Are there going to be screamers?" Sam asked his mom.

"Well, your little cousins might get scared at the loud noise but I don't know if they'll scream," she answered.

"No, not screaming, Mom, screamers! You know, the fireworks that make a squealing sound."

"We call those screamers, Mom," said Derek. "There's also bangers, poppers, boomers, crackers, sizzlers…plus a few more that I forget. You'll see."

"Believe it or not, boys, I've been to plenty of fireworks. More than you, in fact," said Mom.

Before the boys could answer, everyone was startled by an enormous BOOM that shook the ground.

"That was a boomer, Mom!" shouted Sam. "I felt that one inside my chest!"

"I see what you're talking about," laughed Mom, and for what seemed like hours, they all stared wide-eyed as the heavens exploded in color and sound.

On the ride back home, the boys rested their heads in the darkness as their van slowly crept along in the lines of traffic. It seemed as if the entire town was filing out along the same small country road back to their homes. Derek squinted his eyes till they were nearly shut and made the taillights of the other cars look blurry like fire bursts.

"I was talking with your Uncle Drew at dinner," Dad called from the front seat. "He said that we could borrow his big tent if we wanted to try to camp out in the woods behind our house next week once this heat breaks."

"Awesome!" shouted Sam, suddenly alert at the news. "That would be so cool, I love camping!"

"How do you know if you love camping?" sneered Derek. "How many times have you done it – just that one time when you were two? You practically slept through the whole thing."

"Yes, but I loved it!" shouted Sam. "Can we go tomorrow, Dad?"

"No, it's too hot this week, but the weekend should be cooler," Dad replied. "I think there's an empty field on the other side of the creek that Mr. Haskins told me about. He said he's used it as a campsite before and no one minded."

"Honey, isn't that where the…" started Mom, and then she whispered something that the boys couldn't hear from the back seat.

"What?" said Sam. "Isn't that where the what?"

"Mr. Haskins also said that a few years ago, he saw a couple bear cubs running down the hill when he and the land owner were clearing a trail," answered Dad, "but that was a while ago."

"Bears?" asked Sam. "Forget it, I don't like bears. No way."

"I thought it was snakes that you were afraid of," teased Derek.

"Bears too," said Sam. "Snakes and bears, they're both bad. Very bad."

"You're afraid of everything, Sam."

"Be quiet, Derek. You're afraid of the wind and storms."

"All right," said Dad. "Don't worry, they won't bother us if we all keep our food put away and make plenty of noise." He glanced in the mirror back at the boys and chuckled. "I've never seen you two have a problem making noise. I think we'll be fine." Mom smiled and the boys laughed uneasily.

Derek nudged Sam across the seat and leaned over to whisper in his ear. "That's over toward the boulder. Maybe we can get over there during the camping trip."

"No way," said Sam. "I changed my mind. I'm not getting trapped in a mine. I don't want to be like Mr. Haskins' brother and fall in a hole. I might get trapped and eaten by a bear."

"We'll see," answered Derek, and they settled back into their seats and closed their eyes. Soon they had both drifted off to sleep with visions of campfires exploding in the sky and brightly colored bears falling into holes.

SEVEN

THE NIGHT

The heat wave broke by the end of the week just as their dad had predicted. Late Friday afternoon, Dad drove Sam and Derek up an old access road to the field that lay past the woods behind their house. The boys helped gather firewood, and before long, the three were seated around a glowing campfire.

"Mmm, marshmallows. Pass the chocolate, please," said Sam. He squeezed the gooey treat onto a sandwich of graham crackers and chocolate and shoved it into his mouth. "These are so good!"

"Hey Sam, watch this," called Derek.

He reached his roasting stick deep into the bottom of the hot embers and held it there for two seconds. Poof! The white marshmallow on the end of his stick burst into a flaming fireball, glowing in the darkness like a torch.

"On guard!" yelled Derek, and he held his flaming stick out like a swordfighter. He slashed the fiery ball back and forth in the air. It looked like a comet racing across the dark night sky.

"Watch out!" said Sam.

"Derek, that's enough," said Dad. "Your marshmallow is going to fly off and start a brush fire in the field."

"Or burn me to death, that would be even worse," said Sam.

"Yes, that would be worse, you're right," answered Dad.

"Dad, could someone die from falling into a hole?" asked Sam.

"Well, I guess it depends how deep the hole is," replied Dad. "Do you mean like a pit? I guess that could be pretty deep and someone could get badly hurt or killed. You need to make good decisions and stay away from deep holes."

"What about quicksand?" suggested Derek, trying to change the subject. "Someone at school last year told me that in the jungle, there's something called quicksand, and if you step in it, before you know it you're sucked in to your doom."

"We don't live in the jungle, Derek," said Sam. "I don't see any gorillas, do you?"

"No, but there's a snake! Look out!" Derek shouted and pretended to run in panic.

"Where?" screamed Sam as he jumped up in the air.

Derek doubled over in laughter. "Ha! Got you, Sam! That's for tricking me in the creek the other day."

"Not funny, Derek," yelled Sam.

"Okay, boys, relax," said Dad. "Derek, there's no quicksand in Virginia, so you don't need to worry about that. Sam, why are you thinking about falling into deep holes? Did you see one?"

"Well, someone said there are old mines in Virginia, is that true?"

"Virginia is new to me too," answered Dad, "but I think there were coal mines in this part of the country years ago. I'm not sure if they were around here though. You certainly don't want to go around one of those, they're unsafe."

"Mr. Haskins said that…" started Sam, but Derek reached over and kicked his leg hard. He shot his younger brother a fierce look through the firelight.

"What was that?" asked Dad.

"Oh, nothing," Derek chimed in. "Mr. Haskins said to be careful about snakes, and Sam is paranoid about them."

"Well maybe if you didn't always try to scare him, he wouldn't be so worried," suggested Dad. "Okay, let's finish up the smores so we can get things put away."

They picked up the chocolate wrappers and boxes of food from around the fire and carried them and the rest of the supplies over to the van that was parked behind their tent. When everything was put away, Dad took a long stick and spread the remaining burning logs around the fire pit so they'd burn down safely.

"Okay, guys, it's late, let's head into the tent and get ready for bed."

The boys climbed into the tent, pulled off their socks and t-shirts, and slid into their sleeping bags. The air was warm in the darkness. Derek unzipped his sleeping bag halfway down the side so he wouldn't get too hot. Since it was a clear night, Dad pulled back the rain flap from the top of the tent so the breeze could flow through.

They all stared up at the sky from their pillows through the mesh top of the tent. A cloud slowly eased to the west, and the brightness of the moon crept out little by little. Soon the cloud was gone, and a round, yellow moon stared down at them. The creaks and clicks of the woods all around were now cast in a hazy glow by the moonbeams.

"Wow, that's cool," said Derek.

"The man on the moon is shining down on us tonight," whispered Dad.

"What?" said Sam.

"The man on the moon," answered Dad. "See him?"

"What are you talking about, Dad?" asked Derek. "I think you might have been standing a little too close to the fire."

"What, you can't see it?" said Dad. "Look up there. See the dark moon craters and how they kind of look like a face?"

"Oh yeah…you're right, it does kind of look like that," said Derek.

"Where, I don't….oh yeah, I see it," said Sam. "Cool."

"No you don't, you just heard me say that," protested Derek.

"I do so, Derek, it's right there!" shouted Sam.

"Enough," sighed Dad. "Goodnight, boys. I love you."

"Goodnight," yawned Derek.

"Goodnight," said Sam.

They laid in silence for a few moments.

"Dad, are there really bears out here?" asked Sam.

"Goodnight, Sam," said Dad. "We're fine," and he reached over and laid his arm over Sam's shoulder. The warm summer air filled the darkness and the three campers drifted off to sleep listening to a night symphony of crickets and tree frogs.

DEREK'S EYES OPENED WIDE. What was that sound? He looked down and felt his brother's legs draped over the bottom of his sleeping bag and remembered that they were camping. He shoved Sam's legs back over to his sleeping bag and they fell with a thud. Sound asleep as always, marveled Derek.

Then another blood-curdling screech poured out of the darkness. It sounded like a whistle or a weird rooster. Derek had never heard anything like it. It was really loud! Like it was almost inside the tent.

"Whoooo, whoo, whoo, whooooooo!"

Derek sat up in his sleeping bag and looked over for Dad. He could make out his sleeping figure still lying next to Sam. Derek pulled his watch from the side pocket of the tent and pushed the light button. 4:00 AM. Still the middle of the night. But what was that sound?

"Whoooo, whoo, whoo, whoooo!" There it was again. It was right on top of them.

"Dad?" whispered Derek, but he still seemed to be

sound asleep. Maybe that's where Sam got it from, thought Derek.

Scared by the noise but even more curious, Derek eased out of his sleeping bag. The air had grown cool, so he pulled on his sweatshirt and sneakers. He picked up a flashlight, slipped out of the tent, and tiptoed over to the logs around the fire pit and listened. The night was so quiet. The crickets and tree frogs had stopped singing their songs and everything was completely still.

"Whooooo, whoo, whoo, whoooo!" Derek flipped his flashlight on and his eyes followed the beam ten feet up a tree branch above their tent. He found himself staring into two huge bright eyes. It was an owl.

"Whoa," muttered Derek. It looked like a great horned owl. He'd seen a picture of one in the animal book that Uncle Drew had given him on his birthday. He thought about waking up Dad and Sam but decided it would be too hard to stir them out of their slumber.

For a few seconds, they both sat there – the boy looking at the owl who was looking back at the boy. Derek was almost afraid to exhale, as if breathing would send the owl away, or perhaps make it swoop down and grab him with its sharp talons. All that would be left of him would be a pair of empty sneakers.

The owl's feathery neck swiveled quickly to the side as if it read Derek's mind, and it spread its giant wings out wide. With one great thrust, it lifted into the air and flew right over Derek's head. He could hear the feathers pushing against the air, and he ducked down even though the owl was well above him. He tried to follow the bird with his light, but it was gone, eaten up by the trees, and he was alone again in the night.

Derek looked around at the woods in the glow of the moonlight. He reached his hands into the pockets of his sweatshirt to stay warm and realized that something was in there. It was the secret notebook. He'd been too groggy with sleep when he put it on to remember that he had brought it on the trip.

He pulled it out and studied the map pages again under his light. He glanced over at the quiet tent. He looked up at the dark woods. An idea formed in his mind and he wondered. And then, before his thoughts could waver, he stuffed the notebook back in his pocket, gripped his flashlight tight, and stepped through the canopy of trees and into the night.

EIGHT

THE CAVE

E ven in the moonlight, the beam from Derek's flashlight seemed to be swallowed up by the dark only a few yards in front of him as he moved along the trail from the campsite. Everything looked so different at night, but he was pretty sure this route led along the southern edge of the fields and then down to the creek. He could follow the creek west to where they'd seen the boulder and run into those kids.

He was certain that the Virginia Mining Company plaque next to the boulder was connected to the *VMC* on the secret box. The map had shown an entrance to a passageway. He guessed that there must be a cave or something down at the base of the boulder. That was probably where those guys had been playing when he and Sam stumbled upon them.

He thought about the coins – the treasure, as he liked to think of it. Sure, it wouldn't be a huge chest with a mountain of gold and jewels like in pirate stories, but those rare coins would be a treasure none-theless.

The spooky dark branches waved at him as Derek walked along the trail. He tried not to think about what else might be lurking in the woods with him in the middle of the night. Was Dad serious that Mr. Haskins had seen bears? It was fun joking around to scare Sam, but now it didn't seem quite so funny.

He pushed those thoughts out of his mind when he heard the faint gurgles of the creek up ahead, and soon his light rested on the familiar path by the running water and fallen logs. He followed the creek along its dips and curves and soon recognized the small hill topped by the line of pine trees and the boulder.

Derek shined his light on the metal plaque along the boulder once more and compared it to the one in his book. The *V*, *M*, and *C* letter designs matched perfectly. He carefully climbed back up the small ledges of the boulder. They seemed much steeper in the dark.

At the top of the rock he could see the first glimpse of dawn as light slowly formed on the horizon. He thought of Sam and Dad back at the tent and wondered if they had noticed he was gone yet. He knew Dad wouldn't be happy about him going off on his own. Sam would be mad that Derek had left him, even though he probably would have been too much of a scaredy-cat to have come anyway. He wondered if he'd made a bad decision. Dad was always talking to them about making wise decisions. But sometimes that was so boring, thought Derek.

He followed a winding path down the back side of the boulder. When he reached the base, he turned and looked up. The giant rock towered over him and seemed even higher than it had from the top. It was still dark down in the valley, so Derek shined his light along the base of the rock. A narrow shadow was nestled behind a pine tree to his left. He moved his light up and down and saw that the shadow was a large crevice in the rock.

Derek looked over his shoulder. Everything was still quiet except for a few birds beginning to chirp in the faint morning light. He took a deep breath and moved into the cave. He studied the notebook and then looked up at the rock walls that surrounded him in the narrow passageway. The map showed the main tunnel winding all the way underneath the boulder. He seemed to be in the part of the cave where the other boys had been playing. An orange water gun leaned against the wall, and a few empty drink bottles were strewn about. Pretty cool spot, thought Derek, but that wasn't what he was interested in right then.

He examined the map again. A second passageway opened halfway along the main one, and then turned further underground to a small chamber. Derek hoped the coins would be there. He walked further into the cave and scanned the walls for a sign of the other entrance. The rocks were rough and jagged. He wondered what had been used to dig them out many years ago. Probably picks and shovels, or maybe even dynamite, he guessed. Derek looked back and decided that he'd gone too far. He hadn't seen anything to indicate another passageway.

He retraced his steps and inched forward more carefully until he noticed a smooth area along the inner part of the wall. It was only about two feet in diameter, and he'd missed it his first time by. He pushed against the rock with his hands but it was solid. When he tried to kick the wall with his foot, his head bumped something sticking down from the ceiling.

He turned around and felt what seemed like a tree root. It seemed out of place that far underground. Wondering if it might be something else, he gave it a tug, but nothing happened. He reached up again and hung on the wood with both hands, putting all his weight into it. The root, or whatever it was, gave way and Derek crashed to the ground and dropped his flashlight.

"Ouch!" groaned Derek, and he clutched his arm. In the darkness, he felt around the floor until he found his flashlight. He noticed a cool breeze against his face that hadn't been there before. He turned on the light and stared.

Against the other wall was an open hole where the smooth area had been. The second passageway! He reached his arm into the space, and the beam from his flashlight faded around walls and out of sight. He jumped up and squeezed his shoulders through the hole as his heart beat like a jackhammer. Derek couldn't believe that he was this close.

The air was chilled and stale smelling as he stepped into the new tunnel. He pulled the notebook back out and traced his route with his finger. The second passage curved to the right about ten feet and then appeared to go down.

"Down to what?" thought Derek as he walked forward and around the bend. He descended a series of crude stairs in the rock that made a tight spiral. He pressed ahead, feeling for the wall with his free hand.

As he reached the bottom of the stairs, his light revealed a small but open room. The treasure chamber, thought Derek. He looked on the far wall and saw a wooden ledge built over a hole in the rock. It was almost like a shelf that had been cut out of the wall. And sitting on the ledge was a metal box.

"Oh my gosh," whispered Derek, as he imagined what could be in the box.

He jumped when he heard the voices. Kid voices, suddenly echoing through the cave. They were far away but getting louder. Derek had been so excited about following the passageway that he hadn't heard them at first. Now that he did, he moved quickly and climbed up onto the ledge behind the old box to get out of sight. He slid to the back of the ledge and held still for what seemed like a long time. The voices had faded, but he wanted to be sure they were gone.

He peered over at the box, which sat only inches from his nose. Did treasure have a smell? Derek wondered. He didn't think so, but he definitely smelled something odd. He moved his flashlight up near his head and flicked on the light. A dead rat lay right in front of his face.

"Ahh!" screamed Derek, and he jumped back in surprise. As he did, the wooden ledge let out a loud creak and began to wobble. He tried to back up, but the boards began to break under his weight. The whole shelf shifted inward toward the wall, and the box slid backward.

"Oh no!" cried Derek, and he fell through the broken shelf onto a pile of rocks. The old metal box crashed onto its side, barely missing his foot. The lid of the box flew open and dozens of coins spilled out onto the floor right in front of him.

Derek's eyes opened wide and he stared. "The coins!" he exclaimed. He shined his flashlight over the open box. "There must be hundreds of them!" he thought.

Despite his situation, his mind raced with excitement. He picked up the one closest to him and held it under the light. The small coin was a brownish color with a picture of a woman wearing a feather headdress.

Derek's heart skipped a beat. It was an Indian Head cent. He looked along the bottom edge of the coin. "1877," it read.

"No way," whispered Derek. "It *is* a treasure!"

Derek leaned forward to pick up more of the coins when all of a sudden more rocks along the shelf above crumbled down on top of him. His flashlight was knocked to the ground and the small space was enveloped in darkness. Derek gasped. His foot was caught under a heavy rock.

He struggled to move but couldn't. His leg hurt. In the darkness, Derek thought about where he was and started to panic. In a cave. Alone. And no one knew where he was. He listened for the other voices, but he couldn't hear them any longer.

"Help!" Derek cried. "Somebody help me! Help!"

His voice echoed through the rock passageways again and again, but no one called back. Derek closed his eyes and felt very alone. This was not how he wanted his treasure hunt to end.

He wished he hadn't left the campsite alone, that he'd listened to Sam about things being too dangerous. He wished he'd followed Dad's advice to make good choices. He wished he had never found the secret compartment or even heard about the lost coins at all.

NINE

THE TREASURE

S am's nose smelled the morning before his eyes opened to see it. The unmistakable aroma of breakfast on the campfire cut through the cool air and wafted into the tent. His stomach growled loudly, and he crawled out of his sleeping bag and unzipped the tent flap. Dad was cooking eggs and sausage over the fire.

"Good morning, Sleeping Beauty," welcomed Dad.

"Morning," answered Sam. "I'm starving!" The smell of sausages was making his mouth water. He looked around, then added, "Where's Derek?"

"I'm not sure, actually. He was out of the tent when I woke up. I don't like him going on a hike by himself without telling me. Not this far into the woods. I was just getting ready to go look for him. Did he tell you where he was going?"

Sam looked at his dad and then back at the tent, but didn't say anything.

"Sam, is there something you need to tell me?"

"Well, um…"

"Sam, where is your brother?" repeated Dad.

"Well, it's…it's kind of a long story, Dad." Then he explained all that had happened with the coins, the secret compartment, the map and the boulder.

Dad's eyes opened wider and wider as Sam told his story.

"I don't understand why you didn't tell me about all this, Sam. You showed me the wheat penny, why did the rest of it have to be a big secret?"

"Derek said it would be cooler if we found the treasure all by ourselves," Sam tried to explain. Now that he said it aloud it didn't sound like such a great idea. He knew he should have told Dad no matter what Derek said.

"If your brother is hunting around an abandoned mine, that is *very* dangerous, Sam. Mine passageways are notorious for collapsing. I'm trying to let you guys have some freedom to explore the woods on your own, but I need to be able to trust you to do the right thing and tell me things like this. And I need your brother to be responsible enough to know better than to go into a mine. Let's get this food put away quickly so we can go look for him before it's too late."

Sam felt bad. He was glad that Dad had let them have some freedom, some liberty. He thought back to what Mom had said about Patrick Henry and his 'Give me liberty or give me death' speech and gulped. He prayed that Derek was okay.

DEREK LAY TRAPPED under the rubble, deep inside

the cave, surrounded by the treasure of coins, trying not to think about his throbbing foot.

It was ironic, he thought. That was a word that he'd heard his parents and teachers use. He thought it meant that things were the opposite of what you think they should be. It was ironic that he was here next to the lost coins, but yet he really didn't care. He was lost and only wanted to get home.

He wondered how long he'd been stuck in the cave. It seemed like hours, maybe even days. It was so hard to tell in the dark. He wished he'd brought his watch with him from the tent. He started to imagine that he saw the coins dancing around him through the chilly air, but he knew it was just his mind playing tricks on him. He was getting really thirsty.

He thought of his old home and how he never would have had to worry about getting trapped in a cave there. Maybe hit by a truck standing on the busy street corner waiting for the bus, but no caves. He tried to decide which was a better way to go – getting hit by a Mack truck or dying of thirst in a dark cave. Why did they have to move to stupid Virginia anyhow?

Right about the time that he was imagining his death, Derek heard a noise. He tried to focus his mind and held his breath and listened. Yes, there it was again – it sounded like voices.

"Help! Down here! Help me!" screamed Derek as loud as he could. His cries echoed through the cave. The voices seemed to be getting closer, but it was hard to tell. "Heeeelp!"

"Hey, I think it's coming from over here," he heard a voice say in the distance.

"Wow – where did that hole come from? I've never seen that before," came another voice. "Look, there's a tunnel!"

"Down here! I'm down here!" yelled Derek.

The sounds of climbing and scuffling through dirt and rocks came from above Derek's head, until he finally saw a light at the top of the hole he'd fallen into.

"Down here!" called Derek.

"Alex, look at that!" said one of the voices as a bright light blinded Derek's eyes.

"Dude, what are you doing down there?" the voice said. "Wow! Henry, look at all those coins!"

A boy's head appeared in the light at the top of the hole and stared down at Derek. He had dark curly hair that fell down over his ears and wore glasses.

"My leg's stuck under the rocks and I can't move it," moaned Derek. "I think it's broken. I fell down here when the ledge broke through."

The first boy, that the other had called Alex, climbed carefully down into the hole and moved his light onto Derek's leg. "Man, that's gotta hurt. Let me see if I can move that rock." He reached down and tried to roll one of the larger rocks to the side.

"Ahhhh!" screamed Derek in pain. "Stop! Stop!"

"I don't think I can lift it," said Alex. "It's too heavy."

"You have to go get my dad," pleaded Derek. "He'll know what to do." He explained to the boys how he had been camping over in the field on the north side of the creek. Alex agreed to run off and get help. The other boy said he would stay with Derek.

When Alex left the cave, the younger boy climbed back to the edge of the shelf and looked down at Derek.

"I know who you are," he said.

"You do?" answered Derek, confused. He'd been so worried about his leg that he hadn't given much thought to who these kids might be.

"Yeah, you were climbing up there on the Mine Rock a few weeks ago with another kid. Alex and I tried to come over and talk to you with Bear but the two of you raced off like the devil was chasing you. We followed you all the way to the edge of your yard but didn't come in. You live in the house next to Old Man Haskins. I'm Henry, by the way."

"Yeah, that's where we live," said Derek, trying to

piece together this new information in his head. Everything was cloudy after lying in the cave for so long. "Wait a minute, did you say that you have a bear?"

"Yeah, Bear, that's our dog. He's a Newfoundland and is so big and black that everyone calls him Bear."

"Oh," thought Derek, feeling dumb. He wondered why he and Sam had run away in the first place.

"You thought we had a real bear?" asked Henry. "That's ridiculous."

Henry shined his flashlight over to the pile of coins spilling out of the box. "So, did you rob a bank or something?" he asked. "Why are you down there with all those coins? Can I see one?"

Derek handed one of the coins up, and Henry examined it carefully under his light. "Holy mackerel!" he exclaimed. "That's an 1877 Indian Head cent! I have a big coin collection but I've never seen one of these in person before. Do you have any idea how much money that is worth? It's extremely rare!"

"Yeah, it's kind of a long story," answered Derek, and he proceeded to explain to Henry all that had happened.

"That's unbelievable!" yelled Henry. "You're like Indiana Jones in *Raiders of the Lost Ark*! Except for the part when all the bad guys' faces melted away. You're not like that, but the part where he found the gold statue. That was awesome. You're going to be famous!"

Derek laughed, which felt really good. He realized now how scared he had been when no one knew where he was. It was nice to have Henry there to talk with, even though he hardly knew him. He was funny, and it was strange that he and Alex were the kids they'd been running from only a few weeks before.

"Derek!" a voice echoed down into the passageway. It was Dad! Derek breathed a sigh of relief.

Henry hopped up and ran over to the entrance of the chamber. "We're in here!"

Suddenly the chamber was full of noise and activity as Dad, Sam and Alex bounded into the space. Dad's face looked worried when it appeared in the light at the top of the hole.

"Derek, are you okay?" Dad called as he swung his legs over the opening and lowered himself down. "Where are you stuck?" he asked.

Derek pointed to his leg.

"We couldn't move the rocks," Alex shouted down.

"It really hurts, Dad," Derek moaned.

Dad looked at the rocks and assessed the situation. "Alex, come down here next to me. I think if we both lift this rock at the same time, it will move enough for Derek to slide his leg out."

"Yes, sir," said Alex, and he slid back down into the hole. Dad positioned himself next to Derek's head so he could have room to lift, and Alex squatted on the other side.

"Okay, Derek, when we lift the rock, you pull out your leg. Ready?"

Derek nodded, and Dad looked up at Alex.

"Okay, one, two, THREE!" Dad and Alex both grunted and strained at the rock. It lifted a couple of inches off the pile. Derek felt the grip on his leg loosen, and he pulled it out with a shout.

"He's clear! Set it down," said Dad, and they dropped the big rock down with a crack.

Dad bent down and hugged Derek tight and then looked at his leg under the light. He gently put his hand on Derek's foot and tried to move it.

"Owww!" screamed Derek. "I think it's broken."

"It might be," answered Dad, "but I think you'll be all right. We'll have to carry you out of here."

Dad let out a big sigh, wiped his forehead and sat down on the rock next to Derek. He shined his flashlight over to the pile of coins that had spilled out from the metal box and raised his eyebrow.

"So, Son….what have you got here?"

Derek picked up the coin he'd looked at before and

handed it to his dad. "Look, Dad, it's an 1877 Indian Head cent! Can you believe it?"

"Actually, I can't, Derek," admitted Dad. "Sam filled me in on what you two have been up to lately. I'm glad you're safe, but after we get you out of here, we're going to have a talk about what kind of choices you are making when you go off on your own."

Derek touched his sore leg and looked down at the ground sheepishly. He rolled a coin across the dirt and looked back up at his dad.

"I know. I'm sorry, Dad. Thanks for coming."

"What are we going to do with all these coins?" yelled Sam, leaning over the hole from above. "Just look at all this treasure! Somebody call the newspaper! Call the governor! We're rich!"

"Let's work on getting Derek out of here before we alert the press," answered Dad. "Come on, Son, let's get home and then we can think about what to do with these coins."

"Dude, you're going to be a star!" cheered Alex as they helped Derek to his feet.

Derek smiled weakly and looked up at his dad. "A grounded star," he mumbled, as Dad raised him up out of the hole.

TEN

THE MUSEUM

D ad carried Derek out of the cave with some help from the other boys. Alex and Henry promised not to go back to the cave or tell anyone about the coins until the police arrived. Alex explained that they lived in the neighborhood on the other side of the woods, and that they had been playing in the cave ever since they'd found it last summer.

Neither had any idea that there was a treasure hidden within the giant rock. They both had heard stories about the stolen coins, but had figured, like most people around town, that it was just a legend and not really true.

When Dad and Sam got Derek back home, Mom decided that Derek's leg was hurt more than any bandages or antiseptic could fix, so she drove him to the health clinic for an X-ray. It turned out that his ankle was fractured, and he came home later that afternoon on crutches. Normally Derek would have hated being stuck inside in the middle of summer, but it didn't matter much because Mom and Dad grounded him for the entire month of August. Dad said even though they were glad that he was safe, there were still consequences for his poor decisions.

While Derek was at the doctor, Dad called the local police station and explained what the boys had found. The officer on the phone was suspicious that Dad was making up the story of finding the long-lost coins. He made him describe in detail exactly what they'd found and where they found it. He even had Dad tell the story all over again to the curator of the Virginia Museum before anyone wasted their time coming out for a wild goose chase through the woods. The curator found Dad's description of the coins convincing, so he and the police arranged to come out in the morning to see things for themselves.

The next day after breakfast, Dad and Sam walked two officers and the museum curator, Dr. William Evanshade III, back to the cave. They led them through the passageways and showed them the box of coins in the chamber. Since he was grounded, Derek had to stay home, which didn't really seem fair since he was the one who had found the treasure. Sam even tried to argue that his brother should come, but eventually agreed with Dad that it would be hard for Derek to get back to the cave on crutches. Sam told Derek later that when the museum curator looked down into the hole and saw the coins laying there spilled out on the ground, the old man nearly had a heart attack. "My golly!" he exclaimed over and over.

The police and the museum arranged for a crew to comb through the entire cave and surrounding woods to look for any more evidence of stolen artifacts, but they never did find anything else. The police told Dad that the caves in the boulder were, in fact, the remains of an old coal mine, operated by the Virginia Mining Company, or VMC, but that it had been closed down for over fifty years. They ordered the town engineers to send some men in to seal off the entrance to the cave so that no one else could risk getting hurt or trapped like Derek. Mom called it a lawsuit waiting to happen. The boys weren't sure what that meant, but agreed that it was dangerous.

Mr. Haskins wandered over from next door when he saw the police cars to see what all the commotion was about. He told the police all about how the museum security guard, Richard Davis, had once lived in the boys' house.

"I always suspected that he was the culprit," declared Mr. Haskins. "He had those beady eyes, and he stole my mail. Probably stole the coins too. He was shifty, I always said!"

The police learned that before Richard Davis had worked as a security guard at the museum, he worked security for the Virginia Mining Company.

"He would have known all about those secret caves and passageways under the boulder," said Derek. "That explains why he had that box and notebook with VMC written on it. He must have hidden the map for safe keeping in the compartment in the wall."

"I wonder what happened to him?" asked Sam. "Why would he have left it all in the house and the mine?"

"Electrocuted!" barked out Mr. Haskins as he turned and started walking back to his house.

"What?" asked Sam, thinking he must have heard the old man wrong.

"He was zapped!" yelled Mr. Haskins over his shoulder. "His toaster went berserk, or something like that. Or maybe it was his washing machine. Or his oven. He was shifty, I tell ya!"

"Gosh," gulped Sam in disbelief.

* * *

A COUPLE OF WEEKS LATER, Dr. Evanshade called and invited the boys to a private showing of the coin collection at the museum. Despite Derek's punishment, Dad agreed to drive both boys downtown.

When they arrived at the museum, Dr. Evanshade escorted them to a back room marked *Museum Staff Only*, and they saw a wide metal table where the coins were being inspected and catalogued. Derek brought with him the old box and the notebook that he'd found in the secret compartment.

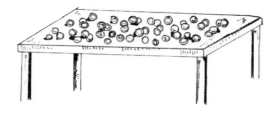

The old curator said "My golly" a few more times and was thrilled with these newest additions to the collection. But the best part of the trip came right before they left.

"Now, gentlemen," said Dr. Evanshade in a serious voice while looking at Derek and Sam. "There is one more item of business before you leave. Since you were the ones who discovered these rare coins, you are subject to a Virginia Antiquities Finder's Fee of ten percent of the recovered goods."

Sam looked confused. "Finder's fee? Does that mean we have to pay a fee for finding the coins?" The situation was getting worse by the minute. "We didn't steal them, sir, we just found them."

"No, no!" laughed Dr. Evanshade. "A finder's fee means the money is coming to you. You get a portion."

"We get a Porsche! Awesome! That's my favorite car!" exclaimed Derek.

Everyone laughed. "No, I don't have any cars for you, I'm afraid," explained Dr. Evanshade. "A portion, young man, a portion. It's your reward!"

Sam's face brightened. A reward! That was almost as good as a Porsche.

"Wait a minute," said Derek. "Ten percent of what, you never said how much all these coins were worth."

"Well, there were over five hundred coins in that metal container that you discovered – five hundred and twenty-three to be exact. Quite an assortment of early American currency, I must say. Back in 1953, it was quite a tragedy when those coins were stolen. In fact, my father, Dr. William Evanshade, Jr., was the museum curator at the time, and as a boy I heard all about the robbery. There were quite a few rare Morgan Silver Dollars, Shield Nickels, Three Cent Nickels, Seated Liberty Dimes and Quarters, and most impressively, there were nearly two dozen uncirculated 1877 Indian Head cents, which, as I think you already know, are extremely rare. Overall, I've valued the collection at just over one hundred thousand dollars!"

"A hundred thousand dollars!" shouted Sam. "Wow – we're rich!"

"Wait a minute, Sam," said Dad, "that's not our money, it's what the coins are worth to the museum."

"But ten percent," said Derek, "of one hundred thousand…" he did a quick calculation in his head. "That's ten thousand dollars?"

"That's correct, Derek," said Dr. Evanshade. "Ten thousand dollars. That's quite a large amount of money for two young men your ages. Congratulations, and thank you again on behalf of the museum and the Commonwealth of Virginia."

The boys each smiled with grins as wide as the Grand Canyon when the curator handed them white envelopes with checks inside and shook their hands. It was like they'd won the lottery! Suddenly, thought Derek, his grounding didn't seem quite so bad.

ELEVEN

THE SUMMER'S END

August pulled to a lazy close, with folks too weary from the humidity to celebrate much. Derek's ankle gradually healed to the point that he didn't need crutches anymore, just a protective boot on his foot. He'd gotten pretty good at hobbling around the house and was ready to get back outside.

He sat on his bed and looked up at the wall where a big new frame hung over his desk. A few days after the police took the coins back to the museum, a newspaper reporter for the *Virginia Times* had interviewed Derek and Sam about the whole discovery. The next week, their picture was on the front page.

"*Local Boys Discover Stolen Coins,*" the headline read.

Below it in smaller print it said, *"Brothers Turn Summer into Real-life Treasure Hunt."*

A picture of them each holding up one of the Indian Head cents filled up the bottom corner of the page.

"Look, Derek," Sam had said, "we're front page news!"

Derek smiled just thinking about it again. It was pretty cool.

Dad had purchased a bunch of extra copies so that they could save them. He took one copy of the front page and had it framed alongside the newspaper headline from August 8, 1953 when the coins had been stolen. In-between the newspaper pages was the Indian Head cent that had been in the box from the secret compartment. Dr. Evanshade had let them keep it since it wasn't officially part of the treasure from the cave and because the boys were so excited about it. It wasn't one of the 1877 coins, but it was still awesome.

Derek decided to give a small part of his reward money to Henry and Alex since they had rescued him from the cave. He figured that if he'd died alone in the cave, it wouldn't matter much how much reward money he had. Dad called that a good first step towards making better decisions. Derek suggested that they hide the reward money in the secret compartment in the wall for safekeeping, but his parents thought a better place would be at the bank in a new college savings account.

SEPTEMBER MEANT that it was time for school to begin – the boys' first time going to school in Virginia. Sam and Derek thought back to all that had happened in just a few short months and marveled. It seemed like just yesterday that they had first set eyes on the creek, climbed up the big boulder, and run from Alex, Henry and a "bear" in the woods.

The two brothers pulled on their backpacks and walked together down the street from their cul-de-sac to wait for the bus. Mom and Dad had agreed to watch from the driveway so that the boys could make a good first impression with their new bus mates. It was nice that the street had little traffic, with not much worry of a truck running them down. The bus, or the yellow chariot as Mom liked to call it, pulled up with a roar and the door opened.

The boys looked back to their house, and Mom and Dad waved. Sam waved back. Derek gave a slight nod, took a deep breath, and carefully hobbled up the steps. He was determined not to fall down and look stupid in front of the new kids. That would definitely not be a good first impression.

Sam stepped on and looked at the driver, a woman with a friendly face, short hair, and a tie-dyed shirt. She said hello and told them to sit wherever they liked today.

As they looked down the aisle at the new faces and tried to decide which seat to take, they heard someone calling their names.

"Hey Derek, Sam! Back here!"

The boys looked down the aisle and saw Henry sitting in a three-seater by himself. Alex was right behind him. Derek and Sam sat down next to the familiar faces.

"Hey guys," Alex called to some other boys sitting across from him, "these are the dudes I was telling you about who found the coins in the cave."

"No way," said an older boy with red hair. "I heard that you got a reward and everything. We saw it in the newspaper. That was you?"

The whole bus turned and stared at Derek and Sam, everyone's eyes fixed on them in awe.

A pretty girl with blond hair in the next seat looked over at Derek with a sparkle in her eyes. "I heard you were trapped in the cave alone. You must have been scared," she said.

"No, not really, but it was pretty wild," said Derek, smiling confidently. "I could have died."

Sam rolled his eyes. "Oh brother," he moaned. He could tell that all this attention was going to go to Derek's head.

The boys spent the rest of the bus ride recounting their adventures and how they had stumbled upon the lost coins. The kids on the bus leaned over their seats and listened to every word and asked all kinds of questions.

Not a bad first impression, thought Derek.

When the bus pulled up to the school, Henry

offered to help Derek with his backpack since his leg was hurt.

"What teacher do you have?" asked Henry.

"Mrs. Lincoln – muller? I think that is how you say it," said Derek.

"No way – that's who I have too! That's radical. Let's go."

Derek was excited to have someone he knew in his class. He turned to Sam as they entered the building. "I'll see you on the way home, Sam, good luck!"

Sam looked a bit uncertain, but then a couple kids from the bus started talking to him more about the coins and led him into the school. He looked over his shoulder and nodded to Derek and smiled as if he'd be all right.

Derek and Henry sat next to each other in their classroom and emptied their backpacks. Mrs. Lincoln-muller was a tall, thin, older woman with big dark-rimmed glasses that made her look like a librarian. She wasn't as old as Mr. Haskins, but she was old.

She stood up in front of the classroom and welcomed everyone back for the new school year.

"The first thing we'll do in fourth grade this year, boys and girls, is talk about what we did on our summer vacation. Now I know that it's hard sometimes to think of anything exciting, but I want each of you to really try to think of your favorite time."

Derek turned and looked at Henry and gave him a sly smile. Henry chuckled.

"Okay, now who would like to go first?" said the teacher.

Derek shot his hand up.

This was going to be fun.

ACKNOWLEDGMENTS

Summer of the Woods was my first book. It grew out of a story I made up for my two oldest boys back in late 2012. We were reading exciting books at bedtime like *The Adventures of Tom Sawyer, The Chronicles of Narnia, Magic Tree House, 20,000 Leagues Under the Sea,* and *Swiss Family Robinson.* I set out to write a new story that my kids would love. Sam and Derek's new home was a lot like ours, since we had recently moved to Richmond from New Jersey. We'd been collecting pennies from different years in little blue books, which led to the idea of the Indian Head cent.

Before long, my little story had turned into an independently published book. My kids and their friends seemed to like it, but when their elementary school picked it for a school-wide reading program, things started to take off. During this same time, our family had been visiting and learning about many of the amazing historical locations around Virginia. I decided to keep writing, combining exciting mystery adventures with local history. *The Virginia Mysteries* series was born.

Over the past few years I've visited dozens of schools and met thousands of young readers. *Summer of the Woods* is now in early development for a feature film. It's been an amazing ride, and I can't wait to see what happens next. Thanks so much for reading.

KEEP READING FOR A PREVIEW OF
MYSTERY ON CHURCH HILL

THE VIRGINIA MYSTERIES BOOK 2

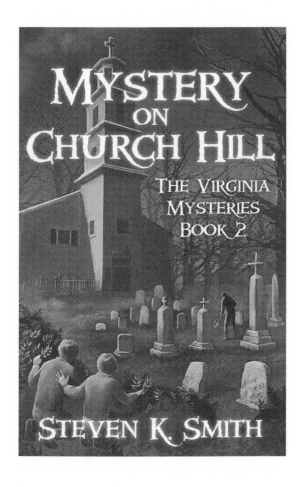

CHAPTER ONE: THE FIELD TRIP

The line inched forward one millimeter at a time. Sam's stomach growled so loudly he thought everyone around him could hear it.

"What's taking so long?" he moaned.

He peered over the counter at the lunch ladies. With robot-like efficiency, they refilled shiny metal containers with stalks of green broccoli and a few hundred over-processed chicken nuggets. It looked kind of gross, but at this point Sam was so hungry, he'd eat just about anything.

Grrrowwllll his stomach cried out again.

He glanced up the line at Caitlin Murphy to see if she noticed. She had a smirk on her face like she knew something, but that was how she always looked, so he couldn't tell if it was because of him.

"Is that organic broccoli?" Caitlin asked one of the lunch ladies through a cloud of steam rising into the air.

Good grief.

Caitlin was always acting like she was too good for everything and smarter than everybody.

The lunch lady ignored her and turned to load more of what the school tried to pass off as food. Sam wasn't so sure it was. He suspected they mixed up dirt and sawdust in the kitchen and pretended it was nutritious. At least that's how it tasted most of the time.

"Let's move, Jackson!"

Sam felt a tray jab him in the back and looked over his shoulder. Billy Maxwell was about to run him over. The lunch line was moving again, and the hungry third graders were getting restless. Perhaps there would be a revolt.

Sam crept forward and held his tray out for the lunch lady to fill his plate. One of the steaming broccoli spears spilled off his tray and onto the floor. It rolled smack onto Caitlin's shoe.

"Eww!" she shrieked. "Sam Jackson, get your food *off* of me!"

"Sorry," said Sam. He reached down to grab the broccoli, but she kicked it across the floor before he could do anything.

"It's organic now, Caitlin!" laughed Billy.

Sam picked up a milk carton from the rack at the end of the line and headed over to his class's third grade table. Lunch was already more than halfway over. His friends were almost finished with their lunches they'd brought from home. Sam sat at the end of the table and scarfed his food down.

The kids were raising a racket. The cafeteria grew louder and louder. Maybe it was the bad food. Or the weather. Ever since last week when the late February days were unseasonably warm, everyone seemed to be acting nuts. Sam's mom said the weather was giving all the kids "spring fever," whatever that was. Maybe if Sam went to the nurse she would give him some real food.

As Sam finished off his second chicken nugget, a voice blasted from the cafeteria PA system. "Third grade! QUIET DOWN!"

It was Ms. Saltwater, the cafeteria monitor. She ruled the cafeteria with an iron fist, the microphone being her weapon of choice.

"It is entirely too LOUD in here, students!"

Since she talked with the microphone so close to her mouth, it sounded more like "RAH RAH RAHHH!"

Sam thought the mic might actually be *in* her

mouth. Maybe she had swallowed it and sounded like that even when she was away from school. He shuddered just thinking about running into Ms. Saltwater in town. Her name was actually Ms. Salwalter, but everyone called her 'Saltwater' because she was so mean.

Like a shark.

Maybe she'd eaten too many of the chicken nuggets – or a kid.

The third grade did not quiet down enough to please Ms. Saltwater. Everyone had to finish their lunch period with their heads down on the tables while she walked up and down the aisles like a prison guard. She swung the microphone back and forth in her hands like one of those batons used for beating people.

Sam peeked up from his arms once when she walked by and he swore she was growling. Brandon was making faces at him from across the table until Ms. Saltwater came up behind him, smacking her hand down on the lunch table.

Bang!

"QUIET!" she yelled.

Yikes.

Eventually the bell rang. Much to Ms. Saltwater's disappointment, the students were released to their classrooms. When Sam's class got back to their desks, his teacher, Mrs. Haperwink, had written something on the whiteboard in big block letters.

"RICHMOND'S HISTORY."

Before she could begin speaking, a hand went up in the back of the room. It was Billy Maxwell.

"Yes, Billy, what is it? I haven't even asked a question yet."

"Are we all going to die?" he shouted.

Everyone burst out laughing.

Billy gave a high five to Brandon Perth who was sitting next to him like they'd just scored a goal.

"Billy, what on earth are you talking about?" Mrs. Haperwink sighed.

"Well, the board says 'Richmond's History,' so I figured we'll all be goners since we live in Richmond!"

More laughter ensued. Brandon clutched his stomach and acted like he was going to roll out of his seat. Mrs. Haperwink, whom everyone but Caitlin called 'Mrs. H,' looked exasperated. She glanced up at the clock like she was counting the minutes left until summer vacation.

In the seat next to Sam, Caitlin raised her hand until Mrs. H gave her a weary nod. "Mrs. Haperwink, are we going to talk about our field trip now? I've been reading about Richmond's history online and in the book I checked out of the library. I'm *very* excited to learn more about it on our trip."

"Thank you, Caitlin, for being so interested in what we're learning," beamed Mrs. H.

Caitlin turned around and gave Billy a look. It was the same one that she'd given Sam in the lunch line.

"Tomorrow," the teacher continued, "we will be visiting St. John's Church in the historic Church Hill section of Richmond. Can anyone tell me what is so special about Church Hill?"

"There's a church there?" shouted Tommy Banks to a shower of chuckles from the class.

Caitlin's hand shot up once again. Thankfully Mrs. H ignored it this time. Sam didn't know if he could bear to hear her superior voice give yet another snotty answer today. He tried to think about the question. For some reason St. John's Church sounded very familiar to him, but he couldn't remember why.

"I'll give you a hint, boys and girls. It has to do with a very famous speech given around the time of the American Revolution."

Sam's thoughts came together all at once. That's it! He raised his hand.

"Sam, do you know the answer?" Mrs. H asked, sounding a bit surprised. Sam and his family had just moved to Virginia the previous summer. As a result, he hadn't learned as much about the local history and places as the rest of the class.

Caitlin squirmed in her seat. She raised her hand higher, not wanting to miss out on the opportunity to show off more of her knowledge.

Sam cleared his throat. "That's where Patrick Henry gave his speech about liberty." Out of the corner of his eye he saw Caitlin lower her hand and sink into her seat like a deflated balloon. "He said, 'Give me liberty or give me death!'"

"See – death! We're all going to die!" Billy yelled again. "We're doomed!" The class busted out laughing again.

"Out in the hallway, Billy!" Mrs. H ordered. "NOW!"

Billy sauntered out of the room with his head held high like he had won the jackpot. Caitlin stuck her tongue out at him as he walked by her desk. Sam just shook his head.

Billy was funny sometimes, but he always went too far. It was just like Sam's older brother, Derek, who was almost eleven and down the hall in fourth grade. He always tried to be a comedian and thought he was God's gift to the world.

Mrs. H turned back to Sam. "That's correct, Sam. Very impressive! Patrick Henry delivered a passionate plea for Virginia to provide troops for the American Revolution against England. It took place during the Second Virginia Convention in 1775. They met in St. John's Church, because at the time it was the only building in Richmond big enough to hold everyone.

"Tomorrow we will take buses to the church, and there may even be a short reenactment of that famous speech. I'd like everyone to read the chapter in your textbook about the revolution, beginning on page 249. To make our trip more meaningful, you'll want to know about several other important people and events that started the revolution."

Sam thought back to why he remembered Patrick Henry. Right after his family moved to Virginia from up north last summer, he and Derek made an amazing discovery. They found an old coin collection that had been stolen from the Virginia museum sixty years earlier. Some of the rarest and most valuable coins were the 1877 Indian Head cents. Since they had a picture of Lady Liberty wearing a feather headdress, it had reminded their mom of Patrick Henry's famous liberty speech given nearby.

Maybe some history does come in handy, decided

Sam, as Mrs. H went over the details of the trip. Most of the history they learned in school seemed so boring, but it might be pretty cool to see the actual place where Patrick Henry gave his speech.

* * *

As they got off the bus that afternoon, Sam told Derek about the plans for his class trip the next day.

"No way!" said his brother. "That sounds cool. I wonder if Patrick Henry's ghost haunts the place."

"I don't think he was buried there, Derek. It's just where he gave the speech."

"Well, keep a look out for his ghost just in case. It's an old church, and you know what they have at old churches."

Derek looked at Sam with a spooky grin.

"What? What do they have at old churches?" Sam couldn't help asking.

Derek leaned into Sam's face, opening his eyes wide. "Graveyards," he whispered, followed by a loud "Boo!"

Sam jumped and Derek ran down the driveway, laughing like a maniac all the way to their house where Mom was waiting on the porch.

Even though Sam knew Derek was just messing

with him, he didn't like talking about ghosts or grave-yards. They scared him. He tried to think about Patrick Henry giving his speech and not about whether he was now a ghost. He was thankful the field trip was during the daytime. Nothing creepy could happen then.

CHAPTER TWO: THE GRAVEYARD

The two yellow school buses chugged up the steep hill, coming to an idle next to the curb. Sam and the rest of his class filed out onto the sidewalk and looked around.

A black wrought-iron fence lined both corners of the block like the edges of a triangle. The fence had sharp decorative points along the top that looked like spears. The kind that always seemed to be waiting to impale someone. Sam imagined trying to climb the iron bars and accidentally slipping and falling onto one of the points and watching his guts spill out. That wouldn't be good.

Below the fence were rows of crusty red bricks. Like everything else he could see, they looked extremely old. That makes sense, thought Sam, since it was back in the 1700s when Patrick Henry spoke here. He peered through the iron bars and up the hill. A stately white steeple poked up from behind a tree. That must be St. John's Church. He eyed the grounds around the church and gulped. They were littered with faded, crooked headstones and tall gray concrete and marble monuments.

It was a cemetery.

"Great," muttered Sam.

"Hey, Jackson!" Billy walked up behind Sam. "You know why they have this fence around the graveyard?"

"No, why?"

"Because people are dying to get in! Hahaha!" laughed Billy.

Sam rolled his eyes.

"Get it, they're *dying* to get in! It's a cemetery!"

"Yeah, I get it. That's hilarious," Sam said in a voice that made it clear he didn't think it was very hilarious.

Mrs. H marched the kids up the steps to the cemetery entrance. They stood in the groups of threes that she had constructed. Somehow Sam had been stuck with both Billy and Caitlin. Definitely not a match made in heaven, as his mom would say. He wasn't sure what was the worst – Billy's jokes, Caitlin's snobbery, or the cemetery. He tried not to look at the tombstones in the grass all around him, but he couldn't help it. Caitlin was acting like a tour guide and kept blabbing about every detail that they passed.

"Look, this person was born in 1723. This one in 1747. Wow – 1711!"

"We get it," said Sam, trying to keep his eyes on the sidewalk. "They're old."

"Hey, Caitlin, ya know why they have fences around graveyards?"

"Shut up, Billy," she retorted and walked around to the back of another big stone monument.

Before Billy could give a comeback, Caitlin shouted to them. "Look at this one, he was a signer of the Declaration of Independence. That is *so* amazing!"

"What would be amazing," said Billy, "is if Mrs. H gave Sam and me *our* independence and moved you out of our group, Caitlin."

This was going to be a long day.

Sam walked up to the gravestone to see what Caitlin was carrying on about. He was still getting used to seeing so many historical things all over the place in Virginia. It was pretty cool that the tombstones were so ancient. Not *ancient* ancient, like the pyramids in Egypt or the Coliseum in Rome. But they were ancient for America.

"George Wythe," Sam read on the stone. He

pronounced the last name with a long 'Y' like '*eye.*' "Did he really sign the Declaration of Independence?"

Caitlin wriggled her nose. "Yes, he did. And his name is pronounced 'with,' Sam. Like, I can't believe that I have to be *with* Billy all day on this field trip."

It wasn't enough that Caitlin knew who this guy was. Of course she had to know how to pronounce his name correctly as well. Caitlin would take any chance she could to act smart.

Sam didn't want to encourage her, but he couldn't help being curious. "Okay, but didn't our book say that Thomas Jefferson wrote the Declaration of Independence?"

Caitlin gave him another look like she couldn't believe he didn't already know the answer. "Thomas Jefferson wrote it, but all the members of the Continental Congress signed it. Including George W-y-the," she explained, dragging out Wythe's last name. "It rhymes with Smith."

Mrs. H called all the groups over to the church entrance. A tour guide wearing funny-looking clothes from colonial times stepped in front of them. Sam looked him over and was immediately grateful not to have lived back then.

The man had navy blue pants that just barely covered his knees with tall white socks that reminded

Sam of a baseball uniform. He wore a yellow vest and a white shirt underneath. It was tied tightly around his neck and had strange ruffly cuffs on his wrists. On top he wore a dark blue coat with lots of gold buttons. Judging by the way he was sweating, the outfit must have been really hot.

The tour guide wore a white wig over his real hair with a ponytail down the back tied in a big bow. It reminded Sam of pictures he'd seen of George Washington, but he'd never thought about George Washington looking so weird.

The oddly dressed tour guide led them through the doors of the old church. The first thing Sam noticed were rows and rows of dark wooden benches. Each bench had a high back separating it from the one behind it. Halfway down the bench was a divider, sectioning them like booths at a restaurant without any tables in the middle. On the end of each row there was a door. When it was shut, the pew looked like a rectangular box.

Sam imagined sitting on the benches for church on Sunday. There weren't any seat cushions, and the backs were angled straight up. He couldn't decide which looked more uncomfortable – the seats or the clothes. Dealing with both at the same time must have been horrible!

The tour guide launched into the full history of St. John's Church, starting with its construction way back in 1741. The class followed him through the aisles to the spot where historians believed Patrick Henry stood when he delivered his 'Give me liberty or give me death' speech. The guide rambled on for what seemed like an hour about why the speech was so important.

Sam stopped listening to the tour guide somewhere around his description of the Second Continental Congress. He was sure it was all very important, but he really needed to use the bathroom. The ride on the bus hadn't been that long, but Billy had brought a giant-sized bottle of sports drink. Unfortunately, Sam had drunk a little too much. There was something about that lemon-lime flavor that made him have to pee like a racehorse.

Sam found his way over to Mrs. H in the back of the group. When he told her his dilemma, she pointed at the side door and whispered for him to come straight back.

Sam found a sign pointing to the left that said 'Restrooms' and headed in that direction. He went through a side door and found himself back outside again. A hodgepodge of gravestones and outbuildings were set on a slope around the church. The black impaling fence surrounded him in all directions.

One building had a sign that read *Gift Shop*. Like everything else, it was made of bricks and dripped of oldness. It had a few signs and shirts for sale in the window. A couple of them said, 'If this be treason, make the most of it – Patrick Henry 1765.' Sam wasn't sure what that meant. He'd have to ask Mrs. H later.

Patrick Henry seemed to be kind of a loudmouth.

He reminded Sam of Caitlin.

Sam walked down the slope and around the corner of the church. He saw a large metal door to what looked like the basement. It was slightly ajar with an unlocked padlock hanging from the doorframe. He hoped this was the way to the bathroom. It didn't really look like it, but the sign had pointed this way and he didn't see anything else.

He reached out and gave the door a tug. It opened with a dim hallway stretching ahead of him. The walls were made of rough stone and a single light bulb hung from a wire on the ceiling.

"This can't be right," mumbled Sam. But he really had to go, so he moved into the hallway. Maybe bathrooms were always in dark basement hallways during colonial times.

Sam wandered through the dark corridor, keeping a hand on the wall to maintain his balance. The stone floor was uneven, and he caught his toe on a couple of rocks that were sticking up in his path. He was about to give up and turn around when he heard something up ahead. He stopped in his tracks, thinking about Patrick Henry's ghost. He listened carefully and heard a man's voice coming from around the bend.

"Are you sure you hit the right spot? I don't see anything," the voice said.

Another man answered. "Yeah, it's right here. I walked it off exactly from upstairs. This wall is right underneath the…what was that crazy phrase?"

"Underneath the one who spoke of liberty," said the other man.

"Right – that one. But there's nothing here. Measure it yourself if you don't trust me."

"If Jerry thinks we messed this up, we'll be dead meat."

"Maybe this Sweeney guy didn't know what he was talking about. Where'd Jerry find that diary, anyway? Up in his attic or something? All that gibberish about the marker. Blah, blah! If I wanted a history lesson, I would've gone to college. This church is, like, 200 years old. Who knows what could have happened during that time?"

Sam pushed his body against the stone wall, afraid to move a muscle. This definitely wasn't the way to the bathroom. He knew he should get out of there, but he was curious to know what these guys were talking about. He didn't recognize the names "Sweeney" or "Jerry." Did something else happen here 200 years ago besides Patrick Henry's speech?

The man started talking again. "Listen, all that stuff is Jerry's job, not ours. He's the fancy historian. We're just supposed to dig." Then the sound of metal against stone echoed down the hall.

Sam took two small steps forward. He leaned around the corner to get a look at the men. They had their backs to him and were working with a crowbar to pry some old stones out of the wall.

This was getting too weird. Sam turned to sneak out. Instead, he smacked hard into a wall and nearly fell over. At least it had felt like a wall. Sam looked up and saw it was actually a man – a big one.

"Where do you think you're going, kid?" the tall man snarled.

Sam couldn't see him very well in the shadowy hallway, but this wasn't one of the men he'd been watching. Sam's cheek ached. He must have smashed his face into one of the big gold buttons on the man's jacket.

"I, uh…" stuttered Sam. "I was looking for the bathroom, but I think I'm lost."

"What are you looking at in there?" The man

stepped back closer to the light bulb. He was dressed in one of the colonial costumes, just like their tour guide.

This guy must work here. He'd know what to do, thought Sam. "There's two men back there digging in the wall. They kind of look like they might be stealing something," Sam explained in a low voice.

"Two guys, huh? Let's go check it out."

Sam turned to leave using the door he'd come in by. He'd seen more than enough for one day. Mrs. H was probably wondering where he'd gone by now. He took a step forward, but the man grabbed his shirt with a jerk.

"Not so fast, kid. You're coming too."

Sam's body tensed. He started sweating as the big man pulled him down the passageway.

"No, really, I've seen enough," Sam cried. He tried to pull away, but his feet were lifted right off the ground. The man seemed to be as strong as a linebacker. They turned the corner and came up behind the other men.

"Making enough noise, you idiots?" yelled the tall man. "You were supposed to be out of here already. There are tours up there!"

Sam felt dizzy. This guy was with the other two? He shouldn't have come down here. What were they going to do to him?

"Who's the kid, Jerry?"

"He was watching you from the hallway. He saw everything, didn't you, kid?" the tall man named Jerry asked.

"No, really! I, I didn't see anything," Sam stammered. "I'm just trying to find the bathroom. I need to get back to my class. Really. I gotta go."

"We'll see about that." Jerry shoved Sam against the wall.

Sam's heart felt like it was about to explode out of his chest. Would Mrs. H hear him if he screamed as loud as he could?

Jerry turned and looked at the hole the other men had dug. "Well, where is it?"

"There's nothing here, Jerry. We followed the directions you told us exactly. Nada. That Sweeney guy must have it wrong."

Jerry smacked the man on the head. "What's the matter with you? Don't use any names in front of the kid!" He turned and glared at Sam.

Sam felt like he was going to puke. This couldn't be happening. He bent over and stared down at his feet. There was a baseball-sized rock against the wall next to him. When he glanced up, the men were all staring at the hole in the wall on the other side of the small room. No one was looking at him.

Almost without thinking, Sam reached down and

picked up the rock. He heaved it at the big man in front of him. Since Jerry was so close, Sam's only choice was to aim for his legs. The rock hit Jerry square in the side of the kneecap, bouncing off with a thud.

"Ahh!" the man screamed, falling onto his other knee.

"What the…" One of the other guys whirled around to see what was going on.

Sam bounced off the crouched man's shoulder and headed for the hallway. He didn't look back at the men.

He just ran.

MYSTERY ON CHURCH HILL

THE VIRGINIA MYSTERIES BOOK 2

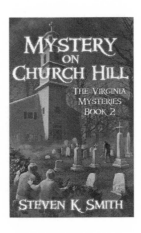

Young brothers Sam and Derek have a knack for uncovering mystery and adventure. When they visit Richmond's St. John's Church for a reenactment of Patrick Henry's famous liberty speech, they stumble upon a hidden piece of history. As the boys and their friends dig deeper, they find clues from America's founding fathers and a secret plot to steal a treasure from our nation's past. Join in the mystery as the search races from the cemeteries of Richmond to the streets of Colonial Williamsburg!

Available now in hardcover, paperback, ebook, and audiobook versions!

ABOUT THE AUTHOR

Steven K. Smith is the author of *The Virginia Mysteries*, *Brother Wars*, and *Final Kingdom* series for middle grade readers. He lives with his wife, three young sons, and a golden retriever in Richmond, Virginia.

For more information, visit:

www.stevenksmith.net

steve@myboys3.com

CHAT

MYBOYS3 PRESS SUPPORTS CHAT

Sam and Derek aren't the only kids who crave adventure. Whether near woods in the country or amidst tall buildings and the busy urban streets of a city, every child needs exciting ways to explore his or her imagination, excel at learning and have fun.

A portion of the proceeds from *The Virginia Mysteries* series will be donated to the great work of **CHAT (Church Hill Activities & Tutoring)**. CHAT is a non-profit group that works with kids in the Church Hill neighborhood of inner-city Richmond, Virginia.

To learn more about CHAT, including opportunities to volunteer or contribute financially, visit **www. chatrichmond.org.**

DID YOU ENJOY SUMMER OF THE WOODS?

WOULD YOU ... REVIEW?

Online reviews are crucial for indie authors like me. They help bring credibility and make books more discoverable by new readers. No matter where you purchased your book, if you could take a few moments and give an honest review at one of the following websites, I'd be so grateful.

Amazon.com
BarnesandNoble.com
Goodreads.com

Thank you and thanks for reading!

Steve

Made in the USA
Coppell, TX
01 December 2019

12146177R00085